A Hard Place

DENNIS KOENIG

FOR WENDY

A HARD PLACE

June 8, 2003. I'm at work and something is wrong, has been wrong for weeks. When a man commands a 24th floor, corner office with ocean view, draws a nipping-at-seven-figure-and-exponentially-rising salary …expense account, bonuses, stock options… when that man, barely 32-years-old, owns a 2.2 mil West Side condo, he should most assuredly not be squandering every bought and paid for hour of every Monday through Friday trying to recall the lineups of every championship baseball team since he was seven years old. That man should be using each iota of skill and energy he, who is I, possesses to further the interests of his benefactor, Park Place Properties Inc., worldwide purveyors and/or developers of industrial and/or commercial real estate. I should be on the horn with

1

Rick Hess, double-talking, triple-crossing, four-flushing. Closing the damn Grange deal. That is what I'm rewarded so lavishly to do and modesty aside, I'm a killer. Driven, obsessed, a hungry cheetah, all survival instinct and bloody flesh in my teeth. But lately? Well, here I am at three P.M. on a Tuesday afternoon…a two-inch stack of memos on my desk, a staff meeting in an hour and all that stalks my mental corridors is the '84 Detroit Tigers. Ah, what a team. Trammell. Whitaker, Gibson, Parrish, Evans, Herndon and…who's on third? In center…dh-ing? What is this!? What am I doing, day after wastrel day? And most frighteningly, what if Bud finds out the voracious Type-A he's been grooming to shoulder his fiefdom has devolved into nothing but a sports trivia desk potato? I've got to cease and stop. Now. I'm an executive, for god's sake. Wasn't Ho Jo at third? Howard Johnson? No, they'd traded him by…

Bzzzzz.

"Ah!"

I jump while sitting. I sit-jump. The buzzer. The private one, wired only to Bud's lair. What does he want? Has his uncanny, traitor-tracking nose whiffed the acrid stench of disloyalty? Will I incur the full-tilt

2

fury of his infamous wrath and be banished to the timecard-punching underworld from whence I once crawled, eking out my career at entry level, chipping in for doughnuts and ruing forever what was lost because I couldn't stop playing a pointless yet really fun game? I don't have to tell you my hands are atremble as I answer that potential down elevator summons.

"Yes, Bu…"

"Howsa Grange deal goin?"

I peekaloo out the big window of my big office. Past Grey Desk Row, beyond the hundred pasty, downtrodden worker bees, all of whom wish they were me. On the far horizon of this white-collar wasteland, framed and backlit in the floor to ceiling bulletproof glass of his Earl of Commerce aerie luminates: The Bud. Makes 56 seem the only age to be. Shirtsleeves rolled up. Moves when standing still. A howitzer with hair. A World Traffic Controller, his telephone headset firmly in place. "Howsa Grange deal going?" Gulp. My only hope is he won't choose this moment to break his 10-year record of never letting me finish a sentence.

"There's a wrinkle with the lease op…"

"Hess. I wanna nail that putzhole good."

3

"…tions."

"Dinner. My place, tonight."

"Tonight? But I have tickets for…"

"Seven sharp. Tie." He's gone.

I'll be at dinner. Bud gets what he wants. Always. He's a single-minded cyclone of self-interest, a tsunami of "me," gleefully crunching all who stand between him and what is rightfully his, which is basically everything. Bud's is the very unscrupulous, robber baron spirit that made this country great. I should hosanna hourly that I have been blessed with a role model of his steamrolling ilk and that he is yet unaware of the recent flights of fancy I've been booking myself on, but…oh, god! Today is the 28th! Bud's quarterly "Asses 'n Elbows" review of productivity is four days hence and I'm a good two dimes short! Even my guru's personal fondness for me will not allow such precedent setting sedition. "Ship shape or ship out," that's his motto…that and "The buck stops in my pocket." If I don't play catch-up and PD quick, I'll be one of those bedraggled desk-bots out there, again, buying my socks 12 pair at a time in a plastic sack. Okay. This is good. I'm frightened. Petrified.

Excellent. Show me a businessman not bullet-riddled with colitic professional anxiety and I'll show you one sorry loser, baby. I have Fay put in a call to Hess. Back to business. Pop some gingko biloba and just do the goddam job. I am zoned. Riding my groove. I'm talking to Hess. I'm thinking...I'm thinking, center field...center field. Ron LeFlore?

I'm at Bud's Reichstag of a house. I'm extremely hungry. Food sits on my plate, but I'm not eating because Bud is talking, has been for an hour and 24 minutes and it's our assignment to be too enthralled to chew. My fellow Slim Fasters are Cassandra, Bud's wife, the Queen of Prozacia, and Lindsay, their daughter and my fiancée. Lindsay is 24 and so beautiful casual observers seldom notice her lips move when she thinks. I do. My fondness for her knows many bounds but the fact that she's my stupendously wealthy boss's only offspring slash eventual heiress is not one of them. I am going to marry her not because I love her nor even because we're comfortably compatible. We will conjoin because it's the smart thing for me to do. Because the business of life is, after all, business. Not that it's all cold calculation. Lindsay happens to be a moderately mischievous minx in the sack, with a particular affinity for the "Soft Yogurt Lick" blow job, so who cares if, when she isn't gumming knob, all she talks about is clothes? She is more than a woman to me, she's a gourmet meal ticket. There is, alas, one minor caveat. Lindsay's orally gifted mouth is identical to Bud's. The same. Exactly.   Budmouth. The horizontal gash I both fear and fear more is also the source of my greatest ecstasy and the incongruity of that has led to much confusion and blurring of lines. For example, a week ago I had a dream in which my career-enhancing airhead and I were engaged in passionate foreplay on my bed. But when I happened to open my eyes it was, to my stunned surprise, not Lindsay writhing beneath me, but Bud. NO! It was Lindsay's body, but Bud's head was atop it. It was Budhead! His eyes were closed and I couldn't tell if he knew it was me who was writhing above him…he was certainly moaning appreciatively…or if he thought I was one of the lithe, 22-year-old "consultants" he often conferred with at their "home offices." I was torn between running away before he assumed his right hand protegee had a thing for him…and staying,

6

because if he had been smitten by my somewhat athletic build and enigmatic hazel eyes, to spurn him could unleash a massive career coronary. Bud then moaned and I became so flustered I bit off his tongue. He yelped, opened his eyes and I wanted to spit Bud's tongue back into his mouth, certain if I did it would magically reattach itself and he'd be so relieved all would be forgiven, and I would actually receive a raise. But I had this urge...it was positively irresistible, to eat his tongue. So I started chewing. It was salty and reminded me of smelt, and Bud wailed and blabbered, "Dib immy ma tum...dib immy ma tum," but I swallowed his tum, defiantly it seemed, and then I started to say something, but I woke up.

Okay, my feelings toward His Highness are somewhat blended. I may not adore him at all moments, truth be told. But the man has shown me how to scale the mountain of life while pushing everyone else off and what more can you ask of anyone? So, when he impulsively reverses field on some project, thereby negating two months of 14-hour days I've spent getting it together, I let it go. When he buzzes me the next day and bellows when the hell am

I going to have that same, supposedly kiboshed, proposal on his desk I say to myself, the greater the man the greater the idiosyncrasies. And when, as right now, that man among men needs to get a few things off his barrel chest, despite the fact that his self-inflating drivel may result in my becoming the first person to ever die of malnutrition in a 10-million-dollar Nazi house, I try very hard to see the larger picture.

"So what do ya do with twelve hundred bibles?"

Ah. The early days. Bud's leaning forward while thinking back, his eyes a celluloid glaze of young buck home movies, starring Bud.

"You go to Kansas."

He jams some rack of lamb down the hatch. It's the most beautiful food I've ever seen.

"God, I was hungry, then."

I know that feeling.

"I wanted me a taste."

Me, too.

He stabs some broccoli, stares it down, momentarily mellow in his memories. Fast as a pickpocket I bare hand some lamb and pop it into my mouth. Nick of time as Bud belches and starts up again.

"I decided where you're honeymooning. Tuscany. June. Villa, servants, car, driver. Day trips to Florence, Siena, the whole Chianti thing. Hundred K, easy, all on Papa Bear. That a sendoff or what?"

Lindsay grins, moonily. She *is* moonily. Human white noise in Donna Karan. In all fairness that could be a result of her father's having decreed every decision of her life. In Budland that's pretty much the price of admission. He makes all my choices and I'm grateful and forever indebted to be pointed and clicked by such a man. Oh, once in a while I do feel I'm not a person anymore, just some papier mâché head stuck on an old toilet paper roll in Bud's elaborate puppet show. But does that matter? I am an orphan from the bad part of the wrong side of the tracks. Raised, only in the sense that while she was around I got taller, by a spinster aunt who spent all her waking hours praying and farting. I grew up upwind and chanting Scripture in a town of four hundred, where the most exciting event of the year was changing the storm windows to screens and seeing how many bugs were dead inside. What, besides who begat Mordecai, did I know? What chance did I have for anything more than some narcoleptic, carpal tunnel syndrome of a career until LL B Money deigned to take me under his armpit? None. Zippo. But now? Thanks to Him? Take my distracted-by-Tigers call to Hess today. Reamed him, thank you. Tossed that clown a cookie on the easements…a dead end, had he encouraged key Planning Commission folk to vote the right way on rent control provisions next week, as Bud had had me do months ago with lovely gift baskets delivered by thousand-dollar whores. God, he's amazing. But the point is Hess took my meaningless bait like a hungry orange roughy and while he was all twisted around patting himself on the back, I boogied with the back end. The *back end*! Gotta be eight, ten mil over time and, remember, I'm not really paying attention. I even asked that mook, in the middle of negotiations, who the unknown Tigers third baseman was. Hess suggested Larry Parrish which was so pathetic I wanted to steal his kid's college fund too, but do you see? Even on autopilot…even while bodyboarding an ocean of useless baseball lore, I'm still kicking ass. I can't not. What was I worried about? I can play bocce all day in the office. Lay down turf and lawn bowl. Doesn't matter. I've achieved Budification.

I'm a freakin' mindless, conscienceless, pushing the legal envelope, raping and pillaging, money making machine. Ooh, Bud's distracted. I grab more meat, sling it down the hatch. He slams the table and honks:

"Nobody gave me shit!!"

And the unchewed lamb wad waterslides halfway down my gullet and takes up residence. I gag. I blanche. I breathlessly flap my arms. My thick-as-a-brick betrothed immediately springs to my rescue. Well, at first she claps and laughs, delightedly because she thinks I'm doing bird imitations. But when my eyes roll back in my head and I mouth the words, "I'm choking to death. Please help me," she leaps into action and pounds my back with a savagery that would impress "Stone Cold" Steve Austin. Seconds thereafter, the death wad slingshots from my mouth and burrows itself into the upsweep of Cassandra's new store-bought "do."

"I took it!"

Now, that's one of the better benefits of being Bud. You're so wrapped around yourself that someone can almost expire in front of you and you don't notice. You just pour some more of your expensive but not necessarily good wine and revel in being you. When you're Bud the world revolves around you. You're the sun. Everything that happens happens because you're shining. This is wonderful. It's a beautiful thing. Truly…be honest…wouldn't you enjoy having only your needs to worry about? No listening to friends tell you they have inoperable tumors, no going to mom's for her disgusting beef loaf because she misses making you feel inadequate…no giving up your Saturday golf game to watch your spastically uncoordinated kid kick himself in the head at soccer. No anything you don't want. It's the perfect state of being. Bud resides there full time. He's left hundred-dollar bills to mark the path and I'm picking them up one by one. Oh, I can feel it. I can truly sense myself becoming more Him and less me every day. Nothing could please me more. However, something is descending upon me. I don't know what it is. I feel light. Lightweight. Polyester. Maybe it's the near-death business…Lindsay's pummeling could've unleashed a rogue chakra…but I grip the arms of my Louis the Somethingth chair, rise and intone as Bud torches a fat Cuban:

"Bathroom."

If, several minutes later, you were in front of Bud's house, you would see a small, stained glass window open. In the Third Reichian, assassin-deterring lights you would see me ease myself through the opening. You would see me lose my balance and half-gainer into a rose bush. You would hear me painfully squawk, as loudly as circumstances permit:

"Yow!"

*

There's nothing like a bad, I mean horrendously putrid tuna melt to piss you off. Then again, maybe it'll kill me which would be nice because cadavers don't have to figure out what the hell is wrong with them. I guess I've gone insane. Blown my mental wad. Flown directly into the cuckoo's nest. I'm in some diner at the far end of the middle of nowhere. Some redneck desert dump where every fellow patron is morbidly obese, consuming food scientifically designed to have exactly no nutritional value and chewing said grub with an open mouth that contains precisely six teeth, none of them touching. How'd I get here? My Saab's outside, nestled between two pickups whose tires are high as an elephant's eye, so I guess I drove. Suitcase in back, so I'm guessing I packed. Where am I going? Damifiknow. How can someone screw up a freaking tuna melt? Bread, cheese, fish, heat. It's idiot proof. It's also white bread when I ordered rye, Swiss cheese so rubbery my big wheel friends could patch their tires with it and tuna so desiccated, the most desperate alley cat would gladly sacrifice two or three lives rather than eat it. I have to go home. NOW. Get in the car and boogie non-stop right back to the twenty-first century. I can still smooth this over. Tell Bud I had some adverse melatonin reaction and reclaim my hard-earned place in the cutthroat scheme of things. Except, I don't think I can. Why? I have no idea. And the knowledge, the absolute crystal ball awareness that I am actively and consciously sabotaging the accomplishments and professional respect that 10 years of avid sucking up, back scratching and ass kissing will bring you in my world, leaves me unfazed. It can't get through. There's some invisible, Pope-mobile shield between me and my former self. Paralysis is what it is. My mind sends a message to my body but all I can do, and with the utmost effort, is almost imperceptibly jiggle the baby toe of my right foot. How can a place call itself a coffee shop and serve instant coffee? Jesus H. McMurray!

"Howsagrub?"

The waitress juts her porcine face inches from mine, so I won't miss even one member of its thundering gaggle of whiteheads. She flicks a cloth that has never seen soap across the counter sending shards of toast and tomato seed flak flying onto the grill where they will be, I'm certain, doused with powdered egg batter, compacted and re-served as the "Roadrunner Scramble." I stare at her chasmic pores. Her hairy chin mole does a belly dance from her gum chewing. I hate her. I hate…the stained nametag says "Verna." Of course, it does. I hate Verna. I hate her more than dogs hate vacuum cleaners, more than Biggie hated Tupac. I hate her almost as much as I hate, at this particular moment, myself.

"How is it? This is how it is."

I palm my hydrogenated joke and chuck it, in a pretty tight spiral. It splats on a rack of rinsed but not washed glasses. Verna stops chewing her gum. I spin off my duct-taped, imitation vinyl stool to find myself face to hairy nipple with a larger than extra-large, tank-topped buttcrack guy.

"Wuz that really nesarry, podner?"

He is, I'd say, six-eight...two-seventy.

"You know, I think it was."

"Our Verna, here works her cute tail off to provide the finest in friendly service to her customers so I think, before payin your tab with extra tip for the cleanup, you might want to give her a nice pology."

He could be two-eighty. Okay. This is simple. A clear choice. I can get my ass kicked, or not. I scan the sneering buttcrack crowd. A couple of oafs drool with anticipation or maybe they just drool all the time. One galumph picks his nose and booger bombs me with it. Maybe a beating won't suffice. I could see one of these fine gentlemen taking in my naturally olive complexion and proclaiming:

"This sumbitch's got niggy blood!"

And they string me up, with my testicles in my mouth and a sign around my neck that proclaims, "How we treet blak tuna melt throers." A prudent man would eat some crow here and beg for seconds, so I offer:

"Verna has B.O. You have B.O. That means body odor which means you stink. You're ugly and you stink. All of you. You're a pack of fart lighting, sheep-screwing, evolutionary rejects who...I don't know if I've mentioned this...stink." Buttcrack stands there, almost hurt. Probably didn't think I knew about the sheep. Then he laughs. Then the whole place laughs, even Verna and the Mexican busboy, who laughs in Spanish. Buttcrack cracks up so much he has to lean on the grimy counter for support.

"Haw haw haw haw haw haw haw."

Then he swings.

*

I've got Saaby heading nowhere so fast my nose stopped bleeding. Joshua trees curtsy from my wind shear. In the mirror, my cheek's the color of a plum and has what could be the imprint of a KKK ring in it. Unh. My ribs. Every breath is an accordion opening in my chest. After Buttcrack bongo'd my face for a spell, I fell to the ground and the entire gang *Riverdanced* me. Interestingly though, I feel...not bad. Perhaps pain is keeping me from dwelling on my psychopathic desire to destroy myself. Maybe malnutrition prevents me from strangling myself to death to knock some sense into me. Mental meltdown? Who cares? Gimme a Tommy Burger with everything. My maladies are my salvation. Distraction equals equilibrium. Perhaps I'll go on a hunger strike. Never eat, again. Watch my body wither away until my pants fall down and my internal organs start feeding on themselves. You know, to feel even better.

*

I might be imagining I'm in a simple yet clean motel room. Asleep between crisp sheets that smell only slightly of bleach. The gooey remains of a takeout meal are scattered around me. My ribs are taped. *Pee Wee's Big Adventure* is on the muted tube. I could be wrong. I could be in my Cal King Super Sleeper at home, dreaming. Everything I've ever experienced could be a dream. Maybe my Farting Aunt Ina was a dream. Maybe Bud as a dream. Maybe I'm just a fleck of dust or a soap bubble floating, floating on wisps of air so light and gentle I will never burst.

*

Desert's gone. Mountains, now. Craggy ravines. Winding, winding. "S" curves with a "C" on the bottom. Totally conked out last night. Ten solid, revivifying hours. Woke up, stepped next door for a micro-ruined Fast Stop burrito, bought eight Tylenol for nine dollars, popped them all and hit the road. Then, when I had no idea where to point the car, I remembered. Everything. Are these gulches? Maybe I'll be dry gulched. I could envision a band of marauding Mexicans chillin' round here playing Yahtzee, puffing cigar butts and waiting for some rich gringo to show up in his stinkin Saab. They rob me, steal my clothes and bury me naked in the sand with just my head sticking out as a buffet for armies of red ants to brunch on. Hey, cool by me. I turned left out of the motel parking lot. Why? Because left was east. Still is I suppose, though who knows anything, anymore. Why east? Time zones. The further east you go the later it is, right? I'm hopeful that will somehow accelerate the aging process and bring the moment of my demise slightly closer because I now realize I'm going to spend every wretched day left to me regretting what I've done even as I continue to do it and can't stop, and the possibility of curtailing that madness, even if only by an hour or two, seems to be all I can possibly cling to. Going downhill, now. The car, that is. I've already bottomed. Back to the valley. Warm. I turn on the air conditioner.

Hours later. Desert, again. Hotter. Got the air on the "Iceberg" setting. Two-laned highway. No curves. Easy driving. Allows me to relax. Deep breathing. Long, deep, calming exhales.

"Hooooooooo."

When you're under stress, perhaps a tad flustered as I now deduce I may have been, you short-breathe. Cuts off oxygen to your noodle, fosters actions that make absolutely no sense, such as attempted suicide by driving east. Ridiculous.

"Hooooooooo."

Oh, my. I feel so much better. Finally relaxing. As if I've had a two-day, full body erection that is slowly drooping into flaccidity. I almost feel I'm me, again.

"Hooooooooo."

This is a window of opportunity that I must quickly

crank open. One final chance to save myself. I will pounce upon this temporary state of sanity to talk some sense into The Idiot Formerly Known As Me:

"Paulie, you've lost your perspective. The big picture."

"Tell me about it."

"Flashback, my friend. Remember your youth? Your lonely, small town childhood? How you dreamed of being part of that exciting larger world? How you would devour newspapers, magazines…science, pop culture, sports, international affairs…? You ate it up. Hungrily."

"To survive."

"Yes. To convince yourself it wouldn't always be the way it was then. It was your life preserver."

"My inner inner tube."

"TV shows, books, movies. From MTV to PBS, Devo to the Golan Heights."

"Laverne and Shirley to black holes."

"You chewed and swallowed, an empty vessel longing to be filled. And what fascinated you most, Paul? What represented to you everything you wanted and didn't have in your minuscule, shoebox life?"

"Business."

"Yes. Those CEO's on the Sunday shows. So assured. So confident, permanent. They knew the answers. In control. Calling the shots. And eventually, by dint of the time-worn success principles of moral amnesia and slyly applied nepotism, you got in and up the escalator, Paul. A made man. Do you really want to give it all up, now?"

"Something's pushing on me. Real hard."

"Push back. Be a man."

"It's…I've lost my compass. My sense of direction. Where is it? Help me!"

"Just stick with the plan, Paulie. It'll all work out. Accomplishment. Success. That's what you want. That's the world's yardstick."

"Yeah, but…"

"No! No 'buts.' You know who says 'but?' Losers. Cab drivers. Party clowns. You want to go through life wearing oversize shoes?"

"I don't know if…"

"Of course, you can. It's a mind over matter matter. Mental manipulation. And who knows more about that than you? Your entire post-pubescence has been one of alpha-managed discipline. You are the Iron Chef of the corporate world. That's why Mr. B. picked you, and no one else, to mentor. He didn't choose Brad 'Road Kill' Radke did he? Nor Donna 'Ice Pick' Capone?"

"No. And she once stabbed a rep who overbid her."

"Yes. That Great Man hand-selected the one stud whose grit and plucky amorality mirrored his own. The Big Guy doesn't make mistakes, Paul. He knows all."

"He's Bud-wiser."

"He truly is. C'mon, truthfully, wouldn't you enjoy being back in the office right, now? Wheeling, dealing, smilingly shafting ol' Rick Hess?"

"I guess."

"You know. And Lindsay. Those lazy Sundays screwing her squirrel brain sideways as she wails. What does she wail, Paulie?"

"'Kiss my tits, Mandingo!'"

"Oh, Paul, everything was sugar sweet, then, and it can be again. Get off the pity pot and reclaim what you've trampled so many people to acquire. The King will understand. He'll curse. He'll throw things. He might even Wally Clep you and dangle you out his window for a while, but in the end, he'll take you back to his burly bosom. Why? You know why."

"Because I make him money."

"Yes. And he makes you money. It's symbiotic. Synchronistic. The natural law of financial ecology. The collusionary glue that holds western civilization together. Do you dare tug on that thread?"

"God, no!"

It's helping. I see it all…in digital video. Who I am and why. My work is my sole identity. Without it I'm nothing, just some old ashtray you store paper clips in. I've got to go back to the only place where I truly exist, to where I *am*. Yes. I'm turning this car around as I silently speak. But…something is fighting me for the wheel. Something strong and morally upright.

"Fight it, Paulie, fight for your future of ease and guaranteed success."

"Get away. I don't want you. Bite off, asshole."

"That's it, Paulie. Do the grown-up thing. There. Yes! You're going the right way now. Going west, young man. It's confusing, I know…this way, that way. Uh, o-kay, where's that disc? It was here, in the glove box, wasn't it? Wasn't it!! I slam the glove box closed, open it, slam it closed again. I won't back down, you hear me? Won't, won't, won't! The glove box door breaks off. There. Mission accomplished. I rest. Yeah. hear me? Won't won't won't! The glove box door breaks off. There. Mission accomplished, I rest. Yeah. Feeling good, now. Thanks, me. Getting the true Paul back. The hard as nails, screwing over everyone he meets, Paul. And that half-man, half-man on the move is not afraid to face the consequences of his recent actions. I'll be the returning prodigal. The comeback kid who's coming back with, if I may be so immodest, a tad more of a quality called character under his imported leather belt. Fear? Ha! I laugh at you. I spit in your face."

Rrrng.

"Aaaaaaaaaaaaaaaaaaah!"

It's my Blackberry!

Rrrng.

It's Bud! He's here, clipped to my waistband!

Rrrng.

My heart is bomping out of my chest! Angina? Is it angina? I'm fibrillating. I'm fibrillating, I know it!

Rrrng.

"Aaaah!"

I rip the demonic black box from my waistband, lower the window and with a strength I never knew I possessed hurl it eight, ten feet into the desert. But it doesn't help. I actually become more tremulous. Epileptic. I'm a paint-mixing machine at the hardware store. I'm ripping the steering column from its moorings. And my head. I'm pounding nails with it. Sweating so much I could swim in my shorts. What's going on? What is it? Ohmigod! I'm still going *back*!

"Aaaaaaah!"

In some basic instinct survival mode I crank the wheel without slowing down. I careen off the road. Saaby is a cat chasing its tail as it spins and sparks in circles. I'm in that Mad Teacup ride at Disneyland. The steering wheel takes over, seems to straighten us out and I start heading back to where I was going before I was going back. Racing east at eighty, a hundred. Running blindly, getting older, getting away. I calm down to the extent that I remember to breathe. I ease off the pedal, take it down to 50. My heart rate slows to that of someone who's just completed a marathon on Mt. Everest. No more listening to me. No returning home. No, no. I never want to feel that toe-curling, hair-whitening sense of utter panic I just endured, ever. Never, ever again.

"Aah! Aah! Aah!!!"

In my rear-view mirror! Something's coming! Homing in on me. A Smart Bomb? Is it a Smart Bomb!? Has Bud declared war? Is it Operation Desert Paul!? Yikes. It's getting bigger. Bigger. A nano-quark ago it was a dot, now it's…a truck. A pickup truck and it's on me like tits on a wet t-shirt. Filling my mirror. It's the Vehicle of the Damned and it wants me. It's *Apocalypse Right This Minute!* Closer. Closer. Oh Jesus, what have I done? I'm sorry. I'm oh, so sorry.

Wannnnnnnh.

"Ach!"

The horn. The Queen Mary's. Kee-rist! Oh, no. What if the driver's one of those murdered guys who come back as skeletons and seek revenge on whoever knocked them off and I'm an innocent dead ringer for who he's after? That's it. That must be it. There's no other sensible, logical explanation. Ohmigod. Ohmigod. Wait. What's that? He's waving. Waving a hand. With skin on it. Hmmm. He could be human. Slight overreaction, I guess. He's waving again. He wants me to pull over.

Wannnnnnh.

Okay, pal. I give him the go-around wave. But…no, he keeps waving me off. Side-waving. Why? He could just pass me.

Wannnnnnh.

This guy's a significant asshole. Why should I pull off the road? Go on, pass me. Pass. I wave him, again. He waves back. No. He's not waving. That's the finger. He's giving me the finger!

Wannnnnnh.

I show him. I honk right back.

Meep.

WANNNNNNNNNNNNH!!

I give him the finger. He re-fingers me. That's it, jerkoff. I slow down. You wanna stay behind me? How slow you willing to go? 50. 45.

Wannnnnnh.

40. 35. 30.

Ump.

What was that? Did he bump me?

Ump.

"Shit! That doofus dick! He bumped me! Oh, you are

picking the wrong guy to pick on. You want to kill me?

Oomp.

Groovy. Let's all croak today.

Wannnnnnnh.

I speed up. Forty. Fifty.

Oomp.

Sixty. Seventy. He's right with me.

Wannnnnnnh.

Eighty-five. Hell's bells! Fuck it! Fuck it all! I brake and…freeze-frame. Hmm. As long as I have a minute, I want to say that if I'm wrong and there is some force out there, some post-crushed-by-pickup answer for your sins thing, that while I wasn't an especially virtuous person I did re-cycle four times, fudged on taxes only when my tracks were completely covered and did not let Myrna Von Schloen suck me off in my aunt's car, even though she wanted to, not only because she wore those gleaming, buzz saw braces on her teeth, but also because I felt, at that particular moment in time, she was emotionally unprepared for an engorged schlong bashing the back of her throat. Okay. I'm ready.

Glllkkk.

He hits me.

Glllllkkkk!

Jimmy Hoffa time. Crinkling, folding, compressing. My foot gets knocked off the brake and the two machines are melded together and lurching...a pair of amorous racoons, and who the hell played third base for the Tigers? The tires are smoking and my door flies open and what's the point? What's the point of it all? *Glllllkkkkk!*

Is there a point? Was there one along the way, that I missed? Was it crystals? Was it Scientology? Oh, I hope not because, frankly, anything that appeals to actors, I...ooh. What's this? What's going on? Huhnh. We've...stopped. Not moving. And I'm...relatively alive. Limbs...working. Seem to be completely unharmed. How about that? I am so humbled. So grateful. I'm gonna beat his ass!

I'm out of the car. I gasp. It's a 180 degrees. I tug hair over my ears because they're sizzling. He hops out of his pickup. Flips his cigarette. We stalk each other. Except...he's a her. Hunh. Ooh! Bad move. Hesitated. She gives me a cowboy boot to the knee. I barely dodge a follow up cookie kick. No choice. I charge. Get her in a bear hug. Ooh. Nice chest. She tries to nail-rake me with a two-inch purple talon. I duck. I'm Lawrence Taylor. Two steps and I bull rush her to the ground. She boot clangs my skull. I wedge her flab-free thigh down, throw my legs over hers. Pretty tight abs. Her chest is heaving so hard it seems her Aerosmith t-shirt'd burst. It does. But I push her arms, push as I used to do the chest press machine at my toney health club. Oh yeah, she's tough. She's not going easy.

"Unnhh!"

She pushes back, baring her tigress fangs. C'mon, Paul you outweigh her by 40 pounds. One more rep, nelly boy. Push, pussy, push.

"Yaaaaang!!"

I bellow. I'm beyond language, beyond human-ness. I'm pure primordial protoplasm with a 300-dollar haircut. I raise up to build momentum and with one hyper-adrenalized thrust drive her arms to the turf. I've done it. I've outmuscled a 120-pound woman! Pinned. Set. Match.

"Okay. Have what you want."

"What?"

"But hear this, Pedro. After, I'm getting my gun. I'll

find you and I will be the bad Lynette. You're in Uruguay I'll be there and when I am, you'll need a change purse to carry your gonads home in."

"Christ."

I lift off her. A lizard leaps from my pocket as I brush desert off me.

"You tried to kill me."

I roll a stone out of my ear. A pretty big one as ear stones go. She hops up. Literally. Without using her arms. In one move, like a gymnast.

"You braked mid-highway. You should pay the ultimate price."

"You were millimeters from my bumper."

"Round here turtle drivers pull off and wave through!"

"I'm not from around here."

"It's common, goddam road sense."

She swirls her hair. Stuff flies out, some of it into my mouth and I start coughing.

"You're a maniac."

"FYI, I happen to be…"

She notices me ogling her chest. Her pouty left nipple is peeking out of the rip in her shirt. An inquisitive toffee peanut. She pulls the shirt off.

"…a professional driver. Big rigs. Cross country and I know from freakin whence I speak."

When tit men dream they see something half this spectacular. She pulls the shirt back on, backwards. She marches over to the Siamese truck and car. I do, too. Her pickup is two feet into my trunk yet seemingly unbruised. Saaby is…shorter.

"Look what you did to my car. It's so…violated."

She hops on the Ford's bumper and bounces. Nada. She bounces some more.

"You gonna help?"

I climb on the bumper. We both bounce. Actually, all four of us if you include her miracle breasts. No dice. She jumps off and paces. She lights a smoke. Engages in something approximating thinking.

"Try startin that turd up."

"Turd? I'll have you know, Consumer Reports rates the Saab 9-5…"

"Start it!"

I amble over to my car. Not too fast. She isn't the boss of me. I get in, turn the ignition. It's a garbage disposal with a spoon in it.

"Piece of crap. What is this Tonka Toy, Swiss?"

"It's Swedish."

"They better stick to meatballs. 'Kay. I'll push us to town."

She stomps over to her Ford.

"You'll push us?"

I follow her as she slides into the pickup's saddle.

"Believe that's what I said."

"Lady, if my Saab, a virtual tank by design, won't start I seriously doubt your rancid pile of rust…"

Her truck vrooms to life.

"Always buy 'Merican, Jose. Now, get in that slop bucket, drop it in neutral…that's the gear with a big "N" on it…and let's amscray."

She bangs her dashboard. The radio comes on. Rock music erupts, a male voice wailing:

"Rock me momma jamma, all night long…"

I move to my car and get in.

"…til the break of day we'll be…"

I put it in neutral.

"…getting it on…"

I lean out the window.

"How far to town?"

"30 miles."

"Take it easy, then make it hard…"

She revs her engine.

"Twenty minutes."

And before I can get my head back in the window, we're off. At warp speed. 20…30…90. I have no control, none whatsoever. I'm completely at the mercy of this trailer park madwoman who is at the moment metallically butt-banging me. In my mirror she's bopping to her tune, "Make it hard!!!"

*

We're at some ragged, paint-peeling yet full-service gas station, which is jammed between a dozen or so ragged, paint-peeling buildings. Five husky guys, all of whom, I'm sure, have had sex with a relative in the last 48 hours, are on the merged Saab's/pickup's bumpers, rocking and swaying them. They're hoo-wee-ing and grab-assing and having a grand ol' time. Then, the cars come apart. Disappointed, da boys go suddenly quiet. They get off the bumper and stand there for a bit. One scratches his chin. Another does some crotch adjusting.

Then, heads down, they sadly disperse.

A few feet away, I'm with that banshee-woman. We are screaming into the opposite ears of another purported female whose name tag reads "Lem." She's middle-aged, burly, in uniform. On her head is a very cool Stetson with a shiny star on it.

"Yes, sheriff. Attempted vehicular homicide."

"Jesus Pete. Gimme a break."

"I want her arrested."

"I'm counterchargin. Attempted dry humpin."

"Before I'd have sex with you, I'd turn gay."

My opponent's mouth, ripe with retort, stops in its tracks. It's owner regards Lem. Lem regards me then measures her words.

"Am I to take it you mean *gay* in the pejorative sense?"

Her righteous eyes step on my neck for a second. I shift, appropriately uncomfortable.

"Just a figure of speech. I'm very upset. She attacked me, and I was already hurting from a set to yesterday and…."

"You make getting into scraps a regular 'curance, do you?"

"I was assaulted. Today. By her."

"I assaulted you, you wouldn't be walkin."

"You want some more of me, lady?"

"Watch what you ask for, Moises. I'll rip off your leg 'n plug your pooper with it."

We take a step toward each other. But Lem gets between us.

"Lose the smack talkin, both of you. Now, Mr...what's your name?"

"Quinlan. Paul."

"You got 'surance, Quinlan?"

"Quinlan's my last name. Yes, I have insurance."

"I know you do, Lyn.

Firing up a smoke, she...Lynette...nods. Lem removes her hat, smooths her razor-sharp crewcut and replaces the chapeau, just so, on her head. Then:

"You take care a yours. You yours."

We stereo her ears with dual dissatisfaction. Lem cuts us off with a referee movement indicating an incomplete pass.

"Lissenup! You start pressing charges and filing suits and countersuits this'll go on til there's world peace, polarizing the tranquility of our rural bliss and makin no one happy but the lawyers and the tabloids, now, am I right?"

From the set of her cop-jaw I suspect she's telling, not asking. Lynette sighs acceptance. I raise my hands, suggesting whatever will settle this is fine by me. Even though it isn't.

Rayno, another name tag says, is now poking around under my car. He's about 20, long-haired yet bald. I step over to him.

"What's the story?"

He stands. Once I had Werner to work on Saaby. Werner is meticulous, perfectionist…Austrian. Now I have someone with a finger to one nostril while he blows snot out the other.

"Um. Allergies. Well, you got yourself a real…"

He frowns, shakes his noggin, snorts deeply and hocks up a loogie the size of a watermelon. He wings it out. It's airborne longer than the first Wright Brothers flight. Werner, incidentally, always wore a lab coat.

"…shitstain."

"Can you get it running?"

"Shoot, I'll be lucky to get her walkin."

He yucks. So does Lynette, almost choking on her cigarette. Being an officer of the law, Lem tries to be above such foolishness but her body trembles and I seem to detect a moistening of the eyes.

"Very funny."

Now, Lem snickers.

"All just kiddin aside, she's hurtin underneath. Uni's doin a loop-de-loop. Rear axle's pointin to hell and back."

"How long to fix it?"

"This ain't the House of Sabe. Hafta send to Phoenix for parts, if they got em, which I figure at less than 50-50. Maybe 50-30. If they do got em, or if they don't but they send to wherever Sabes is made to get em and when they do get em they ship em to us and, hopefully, it's the right parts, then there's the question of do I know where to put em. You with me?"

For some reason I turn to Lem for help.

"He's all we got."

Wonderful.

"All right. If they do 'got em,' and by some miracle you know where to 'put em,' how long then?"

"FedEx won't be by til Tuesday. Humpy Moore's

septic-mobile's comin in then which, trust me, is Priority A and a half, but I get to you, say, Thursday. Two days labor…I can bang out that rear end pretty good, on the house. Primer it up you'll fit pretty regular round here. Figure time for paint dryin, plus what I lose pumpin gas and what not…you'll be layin rubber in five days…a week, guaranteed."

A week. Seven days that are years. I can't do it. I'm an emotional shark. Stop moving, die. I drop a knee to the ground, scoop some dirt and run it through my fingers because it's less painful than what I want to do which is to get a running start and ram my head into that gas pump over there. Wait a minute. Hold everything. There's probably one of those fancy desert resorts in the area. You know, where people come from hundreds of miles away to enjoy sitting in their room for a week because it's so hot if they stepped outside for more than three seconds they'd explode. Sounds good to me. If I'm going off the deep end I may as well do it in a Jacuzzi suite. I'll drink the week away. Cosmopolitan myself to sleep each night. Drunkenly regale my fellow resorters with off-key show tunes and tales of what a big shot I used to be.

What do I care? Let everyone suffer as I am. They can pay for my angst. I'll puke in the pool, piss in my pea soup. I'll be the biggest asshole that place has ever seen and all at off-season rates. Good. Nice to know I can still think straight.

"What, may I ask is the finest…the most upscale …the very highest end, dining and lodging facility in these parts? Money is no object."

Lem kneels next to me. She, commiseratingly, picks up some dirt and sifts it through her fingers.

"Don't got none."

"You must have something. A B&B? Clarion Inn?"

She drops a bear paw around my shoulder.

"There's a Motel 4 up in New Sand, 50 miles of dirt road or so, but the plumbin's shot and there's talk of yellow fever."

Rayno leans over Lem. Like an umpire behind the catcher.

"Widow Peak still lettin out rooms?"

"Widow Peak's dead."

"Hell she is."

"I found the dang body, Rayno. Decomposed for a month. Her ears was stumps."

"This is an A-bomb on my heart. I loved that woman."

He turns away. His shoulders heave. Lem stands, throws her same arm, her empathy arm, around the crushed chrome dome.

"We all did."

Lem is too tough to cry, but she's hurting, too. She and Rayno share a moment of reverent silence for the earless Good Widow. I stand, paw the ground with my feet. The gas pump's right in my sights. Then, Lynette materializes in front of me, holding my suitcase.

"C'mon."

She drags me toward her truck.

"What? Hey."

"This is not admittin responsibility, you hear?"

She shotputs my Florentine suede case into the Ford's rear bed.

"Where are we going?"

"Get in, 'fore I bust your other cheek."

"You didn't even scratch me. My cheek was already bruised."

"Says you. I know my mark."

She opens the passenger door, pushes me in. I'm so

dispirited I allow her. Let someone else take over. Leave it to fate. She slams the door, zips around and slides in. Not that it matters, but:

"Where are we going?"

She starts the engine, guns it as if attempting to grind every valve and piston into fairy dust.

"Better buckle up."

Before I can she floors it.

We flame down the road so fast my nose flattens, and my teeth loosen. My molecules hold hands to keep my face from peeling off. To assuage my fears of a bloody crash, the odds of which I place at approximately 50-30, sweet Lynette offers up some Easy Listening music on the radio.

"....Come on, baby, smash my skull. Come on baby, lunch upon my brain."

And then, some twenty minutes before we left, we're here, wherever that is. We veered onto some dirt rut, Cuisinarted my kidneys for another three minutes and then dove into a half-mile skid before hook sliding to a thankful stop. I leap from that rolling death trap before it starts up again of its own volition. My legs do some kind of anti-gravity wobble. My skin's so wind burned I want to Chap Stick my whole face. I lean on a tree for support.

"Yaq!"

It's a cactus. I pick out needles and try to take in the surroundings. It doesn't matter where I am, of course, which is good, because Lynette's demo of how to get some place if taking a NASA rocket is too slow, has created a blinding dust bowl around us that would soon, I'm sure, make the surrounding 500 miles and possibly several other states eligible for federal disaster assistance.

Someone appears.

"We're here."

From the glow of the cigarette I assume it's Lynette.

"I'm waiting."

"For what?"

"The sonic boom."

"Do everything fast you live longer."

I ponder this cocktail napkin haiku as Lynette steps to the back of the truck. She grabs my suitcase with one hand. It's easy because it's open. And empty.

"My stuff! My clothes. My laptop!"

"What's that you're holdin?"

I'm holding my laptop.

"You're responsible for the loss of every Tommy Hilfiger item in that case."

"Cheap thing musta not been closed right."

"Damn. It was closed. It just wasn't tested for enough g-forces."

"I'm doin you a favor. Shut up."

"What's your next favor? Setting me on fire?"

"I got my Bic. Keep talkin."

She heads somewhere. What else can I do? I follow.

"Where are we?"

"I'm puttin your ass up, though god knows why."

"Hey, I didn't ask you…ummph."

I'd hit something with my nose. Something hard.

"Meet my rig."

The dust abates enough that I can make out the blue and silver, 76-wheel, Rhode-Island-sized product transporting machine and minor league hockey rink. Lynette strokes its metal hide so lovingly you'd think it'd bone up

"'Fightin Lady.' That's what I call her."

"Nothing was ever so aptly named. Do you have any Neosporin?"

I tenderly fondle my nose for cartilage damage. Lynette sneers at this obvious sign of pussiness.

"You gotta be from L.A."

"Oh, you know everything don't you? Why? Why are you so sure out of the hundreds of cities and towns in this vast nation that I'm from Los Angeles? Take me through your thought processes, such as they are."

"L.A. people turn everything that happens into a big soap opera, starring them."

"That is a ridiculously simplistic generalization."

"Then, where you from?"

"Well...L.A. But that does not invalidate my point."

"How'd you get here? Make a wrong turn goin to Spaygo?"

"I'm on vacation. Thought I'd see the country."

"You a white-collar crook? Boogie with the company store? That what was in the suitcase?

"I have never committed a provable crime in my life and I don't have to explain anything to you."

"Just want to know who's sharin my teepee."

"Teepee? You live in a tent?"

"C'mon, yuppie boy."

She clomps forward. I stagger in tow.

"Yuppie. That is such a worn-out cliché."

"You're in worn out country, son."

I stumble.

"And I'd trade in those tasseled loafers for some boots."

I regain my balance and move on. Something looms. I mean, looms. A shadow so big the temperature drops to 110. I halt. Whoa. Whoa!

"Cat got your feet?"

I'm waving off the brown air. Coming ever more clearly into my sights is a house. Tidy. White. A barn to the right of it. But to the left of the house is…a rock. A big rock. A huge, giant Prudential Rock of Ages rock. Maybe 40, 50 feet high and that much around at its base. It sprouts from the ground at a forty-five-degree angle and…it's shaped like a missile…it extends directly over the house and barn. A giant, hovering, Cinzano rock canopy. I'm…I don't know what I am. Silently, as did Ahab's crewman who spotted the great white whale, I point at the massive monolith.

Lynette, following my finger ogles the slab, curiously, as if, perhaps, there's some other even more unlikely object hanging over her domicile. But no, it's just the rock. She shrugs.

"Rent's cheap. Never need air conditionin."

She steps to the front door, opens it. I guess I'm still pointing. I know I'm still standing there.

"Flies're gettin in."

Ten minutes and 54 very short, very hesitant steps later, I enter the dwelling. Its interior isn't too bad, if you're a Peruvian Indian. A sagging-cushioned plaid couch. A Barco-lounger. Actual swag lamp. Packing crate coffee table. An autographed Dale Earnhardt poster provides the artwork. Lynette nods, proudly, to the corner of the room. And there resides the centerpiece, the one absolutely necessary, defining ingredient that truly and forever earns this abode the sobriquet "White Trash Central," a Dolby stereo, picture-in-picture, makes mashed potatoes, washes your car, brand new, 200-inch, bigger than big screen TV. I almost genuflect before it. Though no one is watching it, the tube is on. I imagine it has never been off. Lynette leads me out of the room with the pithy admonition:

"House rules. No feet on the furniture."

She pushes open a door and enters the kitchen. I

enter, also, right after the door swings back and smacks my forehead. A Formica table and chairs. That's about it. Lynette's sniffing into a pot on the stove. I check my watch which reads 3:15. I'm again famished and delighted that these people eat lunch late.

"Suppertime!"

She bellows. Of course. My watch is off. I have it set for the twenty-first century. I collapse in a chair. An old man wanders in with the bon mot:

"Da manure iss gut."

He's about sixty. Burly, strong-looking. Resembles Hemingway, right before Papa blew himself away, I'd surmise from the grimly addled expression on his waffle iron face. A worker, from the bib overalls and the aroma emanating from him that, while not verifying that "da manure iss gut," does attest to its pungency.

A teenage boy materializes from an adjoining hall. I wait for raucous audience applause followed by a wiseass remark because he's virtual Fonzie. Maybe thirteen. Pompadour. Leather jacket. Good combination there, dude. Thermonuclear temperatures and cowhide. You're your own tanning factory. Of course, technically, it is still spring. Pleasant thought. Lynette makes the introductions:

"Henrik, Eddie, this here's Quinlan Paul. He's a Yuppie who smashed into my truck and broke his shitty Swiss car and begged to stay here til it's fixed."

I'm too tired to object. I silently wag a hand. Henrik grunts something. Eddie says:

"Hope that idiot Rayno isn't working on it."

Lynette, in a Jon Waters moment, dons a pink apron. It goes well with the cigarette in her lips and the tattoo I now notice on her right bicep, that proclaims, "Step Off A-hole."

"Bit a help, please."

She hauls the pot to the table. Henrik brings bowls, Eddie the spoons. She ladles out what appears to be some kind of stew. For some reason she yells loudly:

"Sure does smell good, this delicious meal Henrik prepared for us."

Perhaps Henrik's deaf. And...did I hear right? He's the chef? Nice to know hands that shovel cow shit also sliced our dinner ingredients. Lynette offers me an appropriately steaming bowl with gruesome globs of meat in it. Potatoes, carrots, turnips, I think. The rest of them plow into their chuck wagon slop like it's a fast-eating contest, making piggie sounds as they do. My god, what have I come to? Three nights ago I dined at Prama, a new Pacific Rim cafe, with a world famous neurosurgeon and his wife, a university professor who's translating Frida Kahlo's letters for a book. Tonight…look at these people, all slurping in harmony. A band with food for instruments. I study my mush. Its appearance suggests something in a petri dish. Gunmetal gray. Slightly luminous. I sniff it. Eau de feces. No, that's Henrik. I spoon a piece of meat. Check it for rattles. I'm starved so I take a bitty bite. It's good. I assume it's just because I'm so hungry, but I chew, swallow, try some more…damn. This is truly tasty.

"So, Edwardo. How's school?"

Lynette's eyeballing her son and simultaneously jamming food in.

"Fine."

Eddie's jamming, too.

"Everythin goin okay?"

"I guess."

"You guess, or it is?"

"I'm fine, ma."

"Need some help with your homework?"

I bite a carrot to keep from laughing.

"Not really."

"I was pretty good in math and geography. Go on. Ask me any state capital."

"Ma. I'm fine."

"Yeah? Hmm. Okay, then."

Eddie goes back to shoveling. Lynette scans him for a long time. Almost motherly. Then, loudly…

"Sure can't wait for that Peach pie dessert we got waitin for us. Mmmm."

Who is she yelling at? Do they keep some psycho Freddie Krueger cousin in the cellar who will weed-wack me to death when I sleep, tonight? Wait a minute. peach pie? Homemade peach pie? Country peach pie made by the same culinary idiot-savant hands that created this deliriously delicious stew? I can't wait. I'm so excited. I'm…oh my god, I'm, at this very moment, overjoyed. Interesting how food can make you forget your troubles. I'm a shambles, a train wreck at Three Mile Island, yet here I am, all atingle at the thought of pie. Why is that? Pie is not going to solve anything.

After I eat it whatever woes I have will still remain, but *pie,* just the sound of the word is making me drool. Maybe it'll have that wonderful criss cross crust thing. Umm. The hell with it. I'll cry tomorrow. Right now, I just want to dig into this scrumptious mush. Dive into it. Back stroke in it. Savor whatever meager pleasures remain me as long as I can.

Grmmmmmmnnnnnhhh.

I spit out a turnip. What's that? What is that horrid sound?

Grmmmmmmmmmynnnnhhyynnggg.

It's… a groaning. An expanding. Something is being uprooted, maybe. Something really big. Something gargantuan. Why doesn't anyone else notice it? Why are they just sitting there, eating with their mouths open? What is it? What could it be?

Grmmmmynynynygngngng.

It's from above me. Right above. Oh, shitfuckshit!!! It's the rock! Jesus. I'm under a giant rock. And it's falling. The rock is falling. The rock is falling!! I jerk upright, sending my chair flying.

"The rock is falling! The rock is falling!! We're going to die! Run, run everyone!" Eddie cackles. Henrik doesn't. He's now asleep, his head on his chest. Lynette slams her spoon down.

"Jeez Louise. You made me swallow a half-potato, whole."

"The rock is falling! The rock is falling!"

"It ain't freakin fallin, just havin a stretch."

"A stretch?"

"Does it all the time. Tell him, Eddie."

"All the time."

Grmmmmpppphhhmmppphph.

I duck. Yeah, that'll save me.

"What if this time it isn't stretching but preparing to fall?"

"There you go with your L.A. dramedy, again."

"Lynette, that massive piece of stone could be, at this very moment, preparing to compress all our three dimensions into one. You don't know. You can't say for sure."

"Bullpucky."

"L.A.? Do you know any movie stars?"

"No, Eddie. 'Bullpucky?' Is that a scientific term, Lynette? Have you had a geologist out here?"

"I met Christopher Walken once."

"Because, if you haven't…"

"That wasn't Christopher Walken, Eddie."

"It was too, ma. Right, Henrik?"

He opens his eyes for a second.

"Huh?"

"It was that guy from *Fargo*."

I yell out:

"…if you haven't, please listen up! Stand, immediately and, without panicking, remove yourselves from this dwelling before you are crushed, Wile E. Coyote'd, dissolved into nothing more than the silt some local housewife will spend tomorrow sweeping out her back door!"

Lynette bangs her spoon down.

"You stifle yourself, Quinlan Paul! Nobody disrupts the peace of our family bonding supper hour with doomsday scenarios. Not on my watch. You got somethin positive to add to the conversing, such as who that actor we met who wasn't Christopher Walken was, then pitch in. You don't, Velcro it. Now, who wants pie?"

"Me," says Eddie.

"Henrik?"

She pokes the again unconscious fart.

"Pie?"

"Um. Ein bisschen."

He goes back to sleep.

"It was Christopher Walken."

"Was not."

Grrrmmm.

 I don't duck, merely flinch.

"See? She's settlin down. Only time you gotta worry is if you hear, 'Sccllcchh.' I did have a geologist out. A holistic geologist. He said anything but 'Sccllcchh' is just growin pains. That sound like 'Sccllcchh' to you, Mr. Yuppie? Cause it sure didn't to me. So, you want pie or you wanna pee your pants?"

I am peeing my pants, but nothing's coming out.

"Pie."

I retrieve my chair and sit down. Lynette goes to get the pie. As she does, she calls out, loudly, over her shoulder:

"Mmm, mmm, mmm. This fresh peach pie is sure gonna be a lip-smacker."

*

Lynette leads me into the barn. My arms cradle a coffee-blotched Indian blanket and a throw pillow with "Willie Nelson is God" crocheted on it. I sniff. Ah, this is where they keep the manure. We pass five empty horse stalls. The sixth and last one is fixed up. That is to say, it has a cot, a light bulb on a cord nailed into the wall and a shade over the window, if you can call a beach towel featuring *The Little Mermaid* a shade.

"Here you go. Everythin but room service."

"I'll be sure to tell my friends."

I plop on the cot, which is so taut I instantly trampoline back up.

"Nice. No lumps."

"You can use the inside bathroom for showers and personal movements."

A thumping from above. Not a rock-crashing thumping but a thumping, nonetheless.

"What's that?"

"Henrik's room's up there. He ain't exactly light on his feet."

"It keeps getting better."

I lower myself, gingerly, back onto the cot. Hitting it, I quickly grab its sides and manage to stay there. I take stock of my digs. This takes one second. A moose head hangs on the far wall. I know how he feels. Lynette's big-haired head replaces the stag's in my line of sight, his antlers now seeming to grow out of her ears.

"You a crack head?

"No. Why would you even ask that?"

"I know men. You got some kinda troubles."

"I'm sore, I'm exhausted. Can I please go to sleep?"

She studies me as if my face were a map. Then:

"Breakfast's 7:30."

And with that, she spins and exits my guest stall. I close my eyes and drop my head onto the cot. It bounces three progressively smaller times, then settles. I hear her boots fadingly clomping the dirt floor like she'll never give up. It's so good to lie down. I feel for the blanket and pull it over me. I curl up. Ah. I smile as I drift off. Sure was good pie.

"Ah!"

I bolt upright. Where am I? Oh, right, the manger. Middle of the night, and…my arms…. Feel funny. Holy shit! I'm nippled up. Basketball skin! Maybe it's the barn. Animal bacteria. Omigod! Is it Mad Cow?!! No. No, these are just goosebumps, aren't they? Yes.

That's what they are. Because it's cold. I can feel it, now. No, not cold. It's freezing. I'm trembling. Shaking. A James Bond martini. It was so hot a few hours ago. Now, it must be thirty degrees. Twenty. My runny nose is solid snot. This stinky blanket's thin as my hold on reality. Cover the toes! Remember those guys on Everest. My god. What have I done to myself? Is this real? Maybe I died when the pickup hit me and there is a hell and this is it. No. Hell is hot. Hell is this place in the daytime. It could be…this is how it ends. I'm dying. Right now. Good. I want it. I want it over. They can ship my pointless carcass back to L.A., a frozen block of ice in a freight train's refrigerator car. You Know Who will claim the body so he can dice me into cubes to cool his drinks on balmy evenings on his veranda, as he gloats out at his vast acreage, dotted with faux Greek sculptures, and silently vows to never give some ungrateful punk the opportunity of a lifetime.

But even if I survive…if a St. Bernard miraculously lumbers by with rum and honeyed brie, what's the purpose? I'm toast. Gone from everything to nothing in no time flat. I'm a VH-1, one-hit wonder. I'm Vanilla Ice. Literally. Worse, even. Iceman, at least, got to be naked in a book with Madonna before nose diving. Something snuck in, some computer virus of evil, devouring all my mental files and folders, munching away at the reasons I was doing what I was doing until nothing made sense. Until I was numb. Not as numb as I am now, but numb, nonetheless. There's this connectedness, this mountain climber's safety line that attaches us to the world…that makes us a part of things. And it is a thin line, my friends. It's dental floss in a hurricane. It snaps and you're…what? I don't know what. Yes. I do. It's this. It's not knowing what it is. Not knowing what it is, is it. Beware oh ye who feel so self-identified. If it can happen to me, it can happen to you. You too can, after one unguarded instant, find yourself asking, "Puff Daddy? P. Diddy? Diddy?" So, my advice to you, and I'm sadly qualified to give it, is, don't look up. Don't look around. Keep your nose firmly to the grindstone and don't, even for a portion of a fraction of a part of a second, question anything. Accept your lot, even if it has crabgrass, because, if you're not freezing to death in a barn, next to a rock the size of all the things Lindsay doesn't know, the message from one who is, is, it's no fun. It's no fun at all.

I wake up huddled under my blanket and encased in several Hefty Grass and Leaf Bags I'd managed to find. It's light out. Bright. The sun smiles through the Little Mermaid's body, erotically. She's pretty hot. So am I. I'm sweating. No, I'm bathed in sweat. No, I'm drowning in sweat. Plastic bags full of it. I'm a damn Doughboy Pool.

"Branh!"

I thrash out of my own steamy amniotic fluid, fighting for breath. I check my watch, which slides down my clammy arm, as I do. Three o'clock. Wow, it must be three *P.M.* But, I'm still exhausted. Debilitated. Can't move a muscle. I lie back down. My perspiration pool is warm, soothing. A thought hits me and I literally levitate out of bed. Dinnertime!

Shephard's Pie. Every single chef on The Food Network, even Ming Tsai, would kill to claim it as their own. Lynette appreciates it, too. Three times she's foghorned:

"Hot dang! I do love this bitchin Shepherd's Pie!"

It is bitchin. I'm allowing every bite to foreplay on my taste buds before swallowing. Man, I know now. I know why those poor souls balloon to 400 pounds. Chewing...savoring...such a blessed side trip from sordid reality. I should just keep jamming the stuff down. Stock up on Cheeto's and York Patties and anything with the name Sara Lee on it and munch til I crunch. Until I blow up. Explode. Ummm. I love these mashed potatoes. So comforting. I'm so un-miserable.

"It was Christopher Walken, mom."

"Was not, Eddie."

"Was too."

Was not. In fact. I'm more than un-miserable. I feel downright plucky. Spunky, even. Hunh. Amazing what a good night's sleep and a couple of morbidly caloric meals can do for the spirit. I was so down last night. On the ropes and being worked over like some flabby, white heavyweight, but now I find myself coming back swinging. Well, jabbing, anyway. On my toes, dancing...actually wondering if I can't at least get my arms around this Boschian conundrum I find myself in. Despite the elephantine enormity of it, this is merely a problem. The first step to solving a problem is to understand it. Talking to myself almost got me auto-erotically asphyxiated, so that's out. I have to go right brain, here. Logic. Analysis. Sure. That's my thing. The real source of my business success…that and always asking myself right before making crucial decisions, "What would Nixon do?" Questioning, seeing the larger picture, that's Paul country. While others would quibble over specifics, pick nits, I'd search for the gist of the problem, run the fundamental issues through my mind, bring them together at odd angles until a cosmic slot would appear and what seemed to be a square and a circle would become two triangles that fit together like old lovers. Surely, I can find that overview here, given some time. I know it. I believe in…

"Walken!"

"Fargo!"

Gary Oldman, but I'm not telling them. Okay, I think it's clear I need some down time. A sabbatical, as it were. Visine the brain waves. Sure. That's all that's wrong with me. I haven't had a break in years. I'm understandably fried. Chicken -fried with, perhaps, a touch of premature male menopause thrown in. Of course. This is not some life-altering experience I'm going through, it's just exhaustion, which must be dealt with, but there is no need to burn any unnecessary bridges. Don't want to throw out the Bud with the bath water, so…I'll call The Big Guy…tell him I'm taking an extended leave, because the pressure's getting to me. Hahahahahhahahahahaha. I can see him now, contemptuously spitting out, "Gee, maybe we should get you some aromatherapy." "Ice Pick" and "Road Kill" laugh a bit too uproariously at this, while shining Bud's shoes with their tongues, and then take turns carving up my company credit cards. No, no, no Paul, this calls for The Big Lie. *Le Lie Grande.* I have to concoct a tale that's so preposterously absurd it can't possibly have been concocted. Okay. I leave a message at the office, that my aunt…no, no…my beloved grandmama has been taken gravely ill with rickets at her hut in Sri Lanka. Broken hearted, I've flown, then paddled, to her hammock-side, but, as luck would have it, right after I got here, rebel forces sealed off the island and vowed to keep every successful young corporate executive from going back to work until their demands are met. Farfetched? Good. The crazier the better, for, trust me, nobody can utter bald-faced untruths with more conviction than I. Well, excepting tobacco guys, of course. They're the gold standard.

But…okay. This is good. I give myself a break. Travel, relax…R&R. Don't press it. I'll know when the time is right to hop back on that fast track, revivified and eager, once again, to push the ethical professional envelope. Okay. All I have to do now is decide what happens when my poor Saab gets off the disabled list and, assuming I survive my nightly hypothermia death match, I exit this country-western David Lynch movie I'm currently in. Okay. Where do I go? How do I spend my recuperative days and nights in the most spiritually healing manner? These are critical questions. They must be answered. So is this one: Okay, is that Black Forest Cake on the counter?

I savage two large pieces so mouthwatering I wonder what the cost of living is in Bavaria. With a show of tremendous self-control, I manage to resist the unseemly desire to lick my plate. Lynette licks hers, then fires up a smoke, then announces:

"ESPN. Tractor pull finals. Five minutes."

And lopes off to the living room for an evening of entertainment with a message. I address Henrik, who's clearing the table and softly singing, "You Were Always on my Mind," in German.

"Henrik, do you, by any chance get a wireless signal around here?"

"Vass?"

"For the internet."

"Vass?"

I head for the living room. As I reach for the door, it's pushed sharply my way. Already once bitten, as it were, I throw my arms up as an offensive lineman would and take the hit on the elbows.

"Achgh!"

Lynette enters, saying:

"We use dial up, like true Americans."

"How did you hear what I said?"

"Light air. Damn, I'm hungry tonight."

She heads for the counter and the cake.

"I don't have a dial-up account, so maybe I could use your...?"

"Computer? Two words, Quinlan. Internet Piracy."

She breaks off cake with her hand and chomps it down.

"Lynette, I need to get online."

"I got all my business stuff on that computer plus plenty else I don't want you pokin around in. Ixnay, dude."

She opens the refrigerator door.

"Sides, I'm sure you got one a those A-pods that does everything but wash your underwear. Use that."

"I seem to have...misplaced it."

She grabs a carton of milk, guzzles, wipes her chin.

"Tell you what. Get yourself up on that rock. Maybe some satellite's beamin around. Eddie got Russia on his radio up there once. Oh, hell." She grabs the entire remaining cake, throws it on a plate which she grabs, crosses the kitchen and exits for the living room. I rub my elbows.

*

I'm on the rock. I fell and slid off once, climbing up. Rock-burned my belly, as I had to use my hands to hold my laptop up, until I backslid into the barn and, I don't know, compressed both Achilles tendons so badly I feel shorter. But I'm on top now, ready to hope for a miracle. I have to feel around the keyboard for the power button, as it's very, extremely dark. The darkest possible dark. It's darker with my eyes open than with them closed. It's Dead Dark and I realize I'm a bit, you know, scared shitless. They probably have coyotes around here.

"Ow-woooooooh! Owww. Owww. Owww. Ow-wooooooooooooh!"

What in god's name am I doing sitting on a rock in the middle of the night in the middle of the desert! When will I wake up from this nightmare? When, when, when?

"Ow-woooooooo!"

Oh, shut up.

"Keep it down, a bit, Quinlan."

What? Lynette's voice from somewhere. I wasn't even speaking, was I? Is she capable of hearing thoughts? Because if she is...eat me, Lynette! You made this all happen. Thank you very much. I punch the power on. Lights. And a few seconds later...I...am...on. Unbelievable. Something good happened.

"You've got mail."

"Wanh!"

I stifle the impulse to throw the computer to the ground and stomp it worse than the butt-cracks stomped, knowing without a doubt that several, if not all of my messages, are from a certain

Budtheman@aol.com. I do not scan them, but hit Edit, Select All and Delete. Okay, I save "Dirty Moms, Dirty Daughters." I am going to be here a while. I also consider sending a short message to Lindsay. I mean, I should. Nothing fancy, just, "I'm alive, but confused. Working it out. Hope to be back by the time you've completed your summer wardrobe." But I'm afraid if I make any contact with the family, Bud will find out, cyber-track me down and turn my body into a Picasso painting. So…sorry Lindsay. Then, I conduct some business. Arrange to have my utilities turned off, paper and cable stopped. Set up automatic payments for my mortgage, insurance, etc.

This accomplished, I initiate my plan. I will use the internet to find a suitable hideout, where I will gradually return to my old spitfire self. Perhaps one of those Wellness Centers, where you chew grass and have magic stones put on your forehead for eleven hundred dollars a day. Yes. My brain is still functioning. Got it under control. All is not lost, far from it. What seemed an earthquake is merely a violent hiccup. Before I know it, I'll be back at the office, married and living the life I always dreamed of and still want. In fact, the events of the last few days have convinced me I desire what I climbed out of Bud's bathroom window and drove off into the night with my lights off to get away from, even more than I ever knew. But, when I punch in letters for a search, I don't type "Wellness Centers." I don't type "Spas." I, for some reason, type: "Success + Get Me The Hell Away From." Bang! 18,472 hits. There's "Expat.com," and "Get Up'n Go," and "Packing It In" and something called "Bye-Bye Bernie." There are message boards and chat rooms and everything anyone who wants to be anywhere but where he is could desire. It's a lost souls smorgasbord, abuzz with suggestions, hints, tips from veteran cop-outers all over the world. Sanguine advice for anybody planning to tell the little woman, "Hey, we're out of star anise. I better get out of bed and go to the store, right now, even though it's two A.M.," and then flagging down the next one-way red -eye to Katmandu. There are heads-ups on how to change your name, get a phony passport, create a false trail. Pointers on finding work in Finland, leasing apartments in Libya and eating well in Ecuador. I'm seeing, now, there's a vast cadre of seemingly solid, stable male citizens who want to stop. Just stop. Stop making sense. Stop being responsible. Stop going to work and changing the oil and paying the bills. Stop everything. This is remarkable. Contrary to contented appearances, other seemingly ordinary guys, millions from the looks of it, absolutely, completely, definitively HATE THEIR LIVES! Look at this message board...listen to the words: "despondent," "lost," "self-loathing," "on auto-pilot."

Here's this one guy, "Les Than:"

"To the world, I was happy, smiling Les. Coaching Little League, running the Neighborhood Watch program, but every night I'd go into the bathroom, turn the fan on and cry my eyes out because somebody was living my life but it wasn't me." Christ, there must be a thousand guys at this site, all alone, all saying the same thing. Dispossessed. Pretending.

Take Dead Dave:

"In my heart I'm a sailor, a sculptor, but to the world it's just, *You're late again, Cable Guy.*" Shit. Is that what it's about for a man in this world? Living a lie? Selling out your soul, even if you don't have one, for...what? Comfort? To fit in? Is that what I've done? Did I have a dream I didn't know I had because I was consumed by the pursuit of success? Have I now wandered off the common path to pursue something finer? What *is* that finer? Because, if you asked me what I truly desired at this moment, it would be to be back at my job, being focused and organized and banging Lindsay doggy-style and not bookmarking Mother/ Daughter porno sites, which I have to remember to remember to do when I'm done here. No. That's not what I want, it's just what I know. A life of all action and no questions. But it snapped. It's gone, somehow. There's a reason my fingers led me to these websites. They know the truth, all ten of them. These guys are me. I'm unhappy. I've been miserable. There, I've said it. I've run away because I don't want to be what I've been, anymore. What I need is not a vacation or a sabbatical. I wish it were that simple. I want it to be but it's not. I can't turn the car around. I want to. I can't.

I lay back on the still sticky-moist cot. Christ, the things I did for Bud. Gene Kelly couldn't tap dance around the law any better. Bouncing books, winking and nodding, pimping…that's what it was, really, face it, Paul. Christ. You got so many potential clients laid,

Wanda's Escorts awarded you their "Golden Condom" one year. How did I let myself become such scum? Why was it that the more disgustingly I conducted myself, the more pats on the back I got? It's the structure. The system. It's all screwed up. Down is up, right is stupid. Oh! Oh oh oh oh! My god, I'm starting to think I might have a conscience! This is not good. Not at all. Don't you see what that means? I have to create my own thing, my personal moral universe. Make decisions based on what is The True Good and all that freaky Joseph Campbell shit. I can't do it. I'm no hero, just a guy getting by, by getting along. But, *bam*! An image emblazons my brain. In color. It's an epitaph. A head stone set in the ground. On it, it says: "There's only one thing that's really important in life. Unfortunately, I never knew what it was." I raise my eyes, to the deceased's name. It's me. Paul Quinlan, aka Quinlan Paul. I sit up. I blink and my stone is gone. Is this a message? Who sent it? I did. I memo' d me. I self-faxed. Something in me, the best part, is still alive, even if on life support and trying desperately to be heard. And instantaneously, I know. I will never return to life as I've known it to date. Lindsay's vagina is but a fading, memory. I know, also, that there is a destiny for me. Well, I don't know it, but I suspect it. If there is no destiny, then everything makes even less sense than it does now, which is no sense at all. So, I will operate on the premise that I do have a course…a way. It's just overgrown and obscured from non-use. I will search it out. I must find it before I die. Even if I never have a chance to walk it, I must know what it is. That's my purpose, now. My purpose is to find my purpose. I won't give up. I'll fight, damn it. Perched here, on the edge of the abyss, I'll curse the invisible forces that would push me to my spiritual doom. I'll wage war. I'll fight the evil, materialistic, self-promoting me…in the air, on the seas. Intelligently. High-technically. Yes. In whatever, momentary flashes of lucidity I'm blessed with, I will scour the world wide web for guidance. Someone somewhere must have answers for me. Or at least the right questions. Or not. Maybe this is just the first step into some labyrinth of no return. One of those M.C. Escher nightmares, with flights and flights of stairs that all lead nowhere. Maybe it's my fate to whirl around forever in an eternal spin cycle. I don't care. I can't go on. I can't go on. I'll go on. Because, I know something now. Something that will serve as a crutch to lean on when the going isn't. I stare at my laptop. All those websites. All those people silently screaming. I'm not alone.

I awake earlier today. I divine this because Moose's antlers are frosted and when I get out of bed I skid on ice and have to perform an impromptu moonwalk to stay upright. But I'm feeling optimistic, encouraged by what I learned last night. My dilemma is common. It's no more unusual than having a canker sore or hating Kenny G. It is true, misery does love company. If you're a totally rusted out human being, but everyone else is, too, then you're really just an Average Joe, aren't you? So, from now on, whenever I hear some social observer utter words to the effect that the whole world's going down the tubes, I will I find myself saying, "whew," and wiping my brow.

Breakfast. Henrik, now wearing the pink apron, is cleaning up. Lynette and I are at the table. I'm devouring fried eggs, fried potatoes, fried bacon and fried biscuits. Lynette, her cholesterol sufficiently elevated for the morning, sips coffee while she puffs on, what, from the disgustingly crowded ashtray, appears to be her baker's dozenth cigarette of this young day.

"Henrik, this bacon is spectacular. What's the secret?"

"I dunno."

Then, to Lynette:

"We outta lard."

"Put it on the list."

Lard. That's it. Fatty pork cooked in porky fat. Ummm. Oh, oh. Lynette's squinting my way. She stabs her smoke out in an egg yolk, which I'm sure she imagines is my eye.

"Time you started earnin your keep."

I respond through a mouth full of biscuit.

"Wnnh?"

"You're sleepin here, eatin here and lappin up seconds like a butt-lickin dog, I might add. Let's talk recompense."

I swallow my biscuit.

"I assumed I was staying free of charge."

"Why would you 'sume that?"

"Well, you did kidnap me. I concluded you were putting me up to assuage your road rage guilt."

"I got better things to be guilty about than you, Enrico."

"Of that I have no doubt."

"I don't want money, just a help out."

"Which would be?"

"This is the first chunk a off-road time I had in months. Everything's backed up. I gotta get the Fightin gal over to Hollis for tires, which is a full day deal in itself. Then I need ta tune her up, et cetera and so forth. Short 'n long is, I want you to up 'n back my kids to school for the rest of your stay. Maybe do a grocery run, while you're at it."

"*Kids*? How many do you have?"

"Well…there's Eddie, who you've acquainted. And then, there's…"

She rubs her brow. She fumbles for her cigarette pack. She pulls one out and takes her time lighting it.

"…Diana. Who keeps to her room a lot. And the thing is, they go to school in different directions, so you gotta transport one, come back, take the other, come back. Conversely, in the afternoon…"

"You have a daughter?"

"That's what I said, ain't it?"

She bores into me with her eyes, daring me to pursue this questioning. I blink.

"Who's been doing this when you're gone?"

"Henrik. But he flunked his DMV the other day, for fallin asleep on the road test and hittin a cow. So, how 'bout it?"

She puffs her cigarette. I've never seen her nervous. I enjoy it, so I say nothing. She taps a finger on the table. I sip my ebony coffee, which is so strong I should be breaking it off in chunks, then return to my meal, saying, offhandedly, as I do:

"Sure. I'll drive them."

"Good. Hear it?"

"Hmm. Hear what?"

She points upwards.

"The rock. Just spoke its piece."

"It did not."

She grins.

"Funny what you can get used to, ain't it?"

She extinguishes coffin nail number 14. She bellows:

"Diana! Five minutes!"

∗

"No bus, huh?"

"All the other students board here."

She swivels her eyes out her window, signaling a desire for no further conversation. I see she's catching her image in the side mirror. She licks a finger and rubs it on her chin, mistaking a smudge on the glass for a facial blemish. She's, I don't know, 16? Hard to believe she's part of the clan. Got a haughty thing going. She's every girl in high school whose world was somehow diminished because I breathed in it. A true babe. Dusky complexion. Nice legs, not that I'm looking. Oh, the hell I'm not. That plaid uniform skirt...those saddle shoes. Oh, great. In addition to everything else, I've become a pervert, leching after children left in my care. Why don't I just whip it out and ask her to pet it, right now? Let them put me away where I belong. Legally castrate me and let me live out my days in some tiny cell where I'll train rats to tango and swap dirty stories with the foot freak next door as he whacks his dong for the both of us. Christ. If she knew what was on my mind.

"I'm a virgin."

I run the pickup onto the shoulder, then back on the road.

"That's, uh…good."

She's now preening in the window and simultaneously practicing world weary expressions.

"I shall remain unsullied until I have turned dream into reality and become a motion picture mega-star icon, the road to which will begin one day after I graduate, in two years and two months, and go to Los Angeles, leaving this joke place and never returning, ever again, not even when she dies, unless, of course, I need a funny story for Jay Leno."

Kids. They say the darndest things.

"You know, I'm from Los Angeles."

"Her head jerks my way as if I had it on a string. She takes a moment. She smiles. Brushes a stray hair. Speaks offhandedly.

"Do you know any agents?"

"Not really. There was a guy in my condo complex, but he died from eye tuck surgery."

Her mouth inverts, cartoonishly.

"Oh."

Then:

"Stop!"

I clank the brakes. Diana gathers her books. We are

50 yards from a sign that reads, "Brigham School." It's one of those simple, wooden plaques that says the people who put it up are too snooty to have to impress you, but you are, anyway, aren't you? There's a winding, tree-lined driveway that goes up a knoll. Atop it, I can see the top halves of stately buildings. All white, which, I suspect, matches the student population.

"Three o'clock. Right here. Anyone asks, you're my manservant."

She's out of the truck.

"I can drive you up."

"Thank you. I hadn't realized that."

She does a great roll her eyes thing, then slams the door. I watch her, as she nonchalants up the driveway. I figure I'll wait for just the right time to tell her she has the same walk as Lynette.

*

"Just keep on this road, Quinlan."

"It's Paul, Eddie. My first name is Paul."

"Oh."

Our forty minutes and counting drive has been

mostly wordless. It becomes silent, again. After a few more miles:

"So, you're in, what...seventh grade?"

"Fifth."

"Sorry. I took you for about 13."

"I am 13."

"Oh."

O-kay. We cruise along in a cloud of white noise.

"So, how long have you lived out here?"

"Couple years, almost."

"Where'd you come from?"

"Baltimore."

"Never been there."

"Newark. Cleveland. Miami. Lexington. St. Louis. Cleveland, again. Racine. Joplin. Peoria. Scranton."

"Wow."

"Some place up in Canada. I don't remember the name."

"Hunh."

"Here we are."

We pull in front of a large marquee that says "Judge Roy Bean Elementary" at the top and "Junior Goat Milking Contest, Apr. 24" underneath it. Six-year olds are marching up the walk. Ten-year olds. Eight-year olds. And Eddie, as he egresses the truck.

"Thanks for the lift, Paul."

"Thanks for remembering my name, Eddie."

He moves off, blending into the other, younger kids, his leather jacket threatening to explode and his pompadour about a foot higher than the next highest head.

I pop into the local market with Henrik's shopping list. More accurately, as it's 70 miles away, I drive, drive more, stop the truck, get out and stretch, screech and jump back in as a lizard attacks me, drive a whole lot more and then pop. At said food emporium, a warehouse the size and population of Liechtenstein, I pass an hour huddled with employees, other customers and a Native American woman named Lucy Redspot, who has set up a display offering free Eggo Waffle samples, as we all attempt to decipher Henrik's Pig-German-English, gobbledygook shopping list. By a slim plurality, it's decided "Rizz Krok" is Ritz Crackers. There's a "caca" controversy but, after a nine to six vote, we settle on its being cocoa. Mission accomplished, we have a group hug and pat backs, as if we've broken the Jap code and saved Pearl Harbor. I then traverse the 66 six-lane aisles, Sisyphusly leaning into a cart that fills four of them, and has a rear-view mirror, as I garner steroided packages of every single food item on the American Heart Association's warning list. Then, with 84 rolls of toilet paper riding shotgun, I drive in circles for two hours before finding myself miraculously returned to Rocky Top, where, in his own, sly manner of both greeting me and expressing appreciation that I didn't forget his 40-pound chunk of lard, Henrik says:

"She sed give you deez."

Whereupon, he hands me a pile of clothing borrowed from the Calcutta Goodwill bin, with some wizened work shoes on top.

"Whose things are these. Yours?

"Ja. Und hers."

And so it was that bedecked in, not my usual designer-logo'd attire, but overalls a foot too wide and bottoming at mid-calf, a stretched in the chest t-shirt that proclaimed "Truck Drivers Do It With Air Brakes" and *Brother Where Art Thou* jodhpurs, I passed the next days chauffeuring, marketing, and jamming dead farm animals down my throat, and my nights engaged in incessant, obsessive web plundering. While no life-changing apparitions had yet filled my monitor, I was no longer a victim. I was doing something about my situation. Plumbing my magic box of chips and semiconductors. There, all the wisdom of the world was at my disposal, and, now that I had disciplined myself to one hour of Free Cell nightly, I was sure that, if I just kept clicking, I would unearth an answer to the question I couldn't seem to form. Well, I wasn't certain, I was hopeful, and hope is a lifeboat. I needed hope the way Henrik needed lard.

*

Lynette deduced her rig lacked more than a tune-up. Something about something called ooh-joints. In replacing them, she found something else out of whack and this went on and on, so, pretty much all I viewed of her *Hooters*-waitress body, except at meals, was a pair of boots, in a pile of cigarette butts, sticking out from under Fightin Lady. One day, as I returned from my driving chores, Lynette was engaged in some major vehicle re-do. Henrik was assisting, manning a hoist thing that had lifted the entire motor housing up. Directly below it, Lynette was on her back half down in the engine well and she said:

"Latch the winch down, Henrik. Easy. Or I'll be wearin that block for a navel ring."

"Ja."

No sooner had he replied, than the cable snapped. Broke right off. The engine released, fell. But, before I could gasp and turn away in horror, Henrik caught it. He caught the engine in mid-air! He slapped his ham hock, peasant hands on the sides of it, like he was playing an accordion and held it. And then, still controlling this thing that must've weighed 400 pounds, the sexagenarian Samson, taciturn as a wooden Indian, carefully set the engine on the ground. And Lynette, completely unaware of what had transpired, growled:

"Slip me a five-eighths on the ratchet."

And Henrik fumbled around in the toolbox and found the socket and clipped it onto the wrench and handed it to Lynette's hand, which was reaching out from what should have been her gravesite.

*

My transit time with Eddie continued to be mostly a silent movie. On the rare occasion Diana would deign to speak, it was invariably to express disgust with Lynette and everything else in her soon-to-be-discarded "country bumpkin lifestyle." Henrik grunted a lot. Lynette took shots at me and I returned fire. But this was not an uneventful period. I was not lying fallow because, if I hadn't developed black lung from inhaling Lynette's coffin nails, my future was bright. Radiant. Because, one, Rayno informed me my car was ready and, two, joy of joys, my intrepid cyber-trekking had paid off...had taken my hand and led me to a verdant glen where all is simple beauty and a gentle zephyr soothes the aching brow. Where to ask a question is to have it answered. Where all is as it should be. Yes, I was off to see...

"The Bog What?"

She's hosing down her rig. I follow her, trying not to get sprayed.

"Bhogwan, Lynette. The Bhogwan Bhogwan. The Bhogwan Bhogwan Institute of Eternal Sublimity, in Bhogwan, South Carolina. That's where I'm going. My car is roadworthy and I'll be departing tomorrow."

"No more La-La?"

"No. You see…I can reveal this, now, because I'm on the road to reinvention…recently, even though I make scads of money and have a gorgeous woman in love with me, I've become very confused about and disillusioned with my direction in life."

"Bein rich and well-screwed could make the best of us take pause."

"Fortunately, the Bhogwan is going to clear everything up for me."

"I'm sure he is."

She throws the hose down. It snakes around and I have to hopscotch it.

"So, what's sublimity goin for these days?"

"It's free. Totally. You just make an initial 30,000-dollar contribution and you get a mat and all the rice you can eat, forever."

"Live 900 years, that's one hot deal."

She pulls a mop from a bucket of soapy water.

"Please, no cynicism, Lynette. The Bhogwan is a great man. He teaches that paradise is right here on earth. All we have to do is simplify, rid ourselves of distractions, possessions, and then, with his loving, vision-quest guidance we will be raised to an existence of complete, harmonic joyfulness."

"Right."

She begins mopping the side of the rig.

"And Mr. Mogban ain't got 20 mil stashed offshore, I'll eat his turban."

"He doesn't wear a turban."

She stops mopping and turns to me.

"Son, your only problem is, you had everything too easy."

"You don't know enough about me to say that."

"Livin the life of Pat Riley, ain't enough? You need continuous, non-stop, every moment of the day and night joy? Gimme a damn break."

She runs a rag over a grease spot.

"It's so easy, isn't it, to ridicule another's internal anguish?"

"You don't know what anguish is."

She snatches the hose. Rinses soap off the truck.

"Don't give me that attitude. You've got some scabs I could pick, if I wanted."

She stops scrubbing, gives me the Lem jaw.

"I was you, I'd be choosin my next words real careful."

"Take Diana…"

"I gave warnin."

She turns the hose on me.

"Hey!"

"You don't know enough about me, neither, Quinlan Paul!!"

*

"This here's the fly in the soap."

Rayno holds up a broken off piece of metal.

"A cotter pin?"

"No. A cotter pin is what they sent. But, what I asked 'em for was a ka-jarta. Ka…jar…ta. Shame, cause the rest of the car's A-one kosher, ready to go."

Lynette drove me here. We shared not a word the entire four seconds the speed of sound trip took, which didn't matter to me because I was high on life. Amped on my joy-filled future with the beloved and benevolent Bhogwan, excitedly anticipating the cross-country pilgrimage to the site of my reborn-ness. But now there's a bump in the road. Or a lump…and its name is…

"Rayno, it looks the same to me. Can't you use the cotter pin?"

"Ain't the same. Ka-jarta's two millimeters thicker."

"That's close enough. Just put it in."

"And have it work free and fling the transaxle up the floorboard, into your left ear and out your right? That ain't real good for business."

"Look, you said my car would be ready, today."

"I didn't know I had the wrong part, when we conversed. I couldn't try implantin the thingy til late last night, cause a funeral passed through and I had to gas up 74 cars and two hearses. The deceased was twins. But, per our policy at Winger Gas and Precision Repair, any dissatisfaction, customer's entitled to a free Garth Brooks bobby-head doll, and at no cost."

"I don't want a bobby-head doll. I want my car."

"That might take a while."

"Unacceptable response. Try, again."

"Some disgruntled Swede blew up the Ka-jarta makin plant in…I think it's Sweden, so none are comin in. The ones that are in, on old junkers and what not, they been all plucked clean."

"I don't want to hear this, Rayno."

"I'll find the part, Mr. Paul, won't sleep easy til I do, but I can't say when. Hey, saw some clubs in your trunk. You wanna golf, sometime?"

"I want to leave, Rayno. With my car. Put the cotter pin in and I'll take my chances."

"No-can-do. A mechanic puts a knowingly unsafe vehicle on the road's no better'n a murder waiting to happen."

"Then sell me the pin and I'll do it, myself."

"No-can, again, Mr. Paul."

"Then, I'll take the car. Tow it out to Lynette's."

"So you can find a cotter pin and stick it in? No way."

"Rayno, unless I'm allowed to remove my automobile from these premises, I'll call the sheriff."

"And I'll chain myself to the Sabe, if I have to."

I grab the phone.

"What's Lem's number?"

"Five."

"Five? That's it?"

"Used to be six, but she was gettin obscene calls."

I punch the grease-blackened "five" on the phone.

"I'm going to have her here in two minutes. In four, you will be towing my car. Don't expect a tip."

Seven hours later, Lem, having had to intercede in a "pot-bellied pig custody thing," has just arrived. She's sipping coffee from her steamy, metal "Calgary Stampede" mug.

"So, you feel no responsibility to your fellow man? Man meaning mankind, not just men."

"I don't believe this. You're taking Rayno's side?"

"I'm on the side of right. That's my job."

Rayno, seated at the desk, fumbles with some paperwork, so as to not appear to be rubbing it in, which he is.

"Sooner or later, Rayno'll get your whatsit…"

"Ka-jarta."

"Thanks, Rayno. And when he does, you'll be back on the road, again, conscience-clear in the knowledge your vehicle represents no undue danger to other highway denizens."

"What if it takes months…years?"

"Now, you don't want no negative self-fulfillin prophecy. Just as likely, you'll be on the road in a few days."

"Glass could be half-full, Mr. Paul."

"Well put, Rayno. And everything comes to he who waits. He meaning she also."

"Amen, Lem."

"I...feel dizzy."

I sink onto a chair.

"He plays golf, Lem."

"That right, Mr. Paul? What's your handicap?"

"I don't play, anymore."

"But, when you did?"

"Six...seven."

"Hoo! Got us a regular Champagne Tony Lema here, Rayno."

"We tee it up every Tuesday and Thursday, Mr. Paul. Been needin a fourth since Han Lee fell in the well.

"Are you cryin, Mr. Paul?"

"No."

"I know how it is, Mr. Paul. Sick dogs and cars just break your heart."

"I'm not crying, Lem."

"The man's broken. Avert eyes, Rayno."

"Ten-four."

They both turn their backs to me, which touches me and makes me not cry even harder.

*

"Forget your toothbrush?"

Lynette has opened her front door to find me standing there. If expressions could kill, I'd be dead and mutilated and the earth around me scorched for 800 miles.

"I need to check back in."

She leans against the door jam and crosses her arms.

"Do tell."

Before Rayno had transported me back to hell on earth, I'd blubberingly requested a few minutes alone with Saaby. Seeing her in the dank, oily repair bay, I almost wept. Her rear end was pounded out, the bumper half-straightened and the damaged area filled and primed with, fittingly, blood-colored paint. Ah, my wounded friend, I feel your pain. I know it seems foolish to keep everything on hold for the sake of a car, but there is an excellent reason why I have. I don't, in keeping with my current, besotted, mind-frame, have a clue what that reason is, but it has something to do with identity.

I could've upgraded to any car on the market. True luxury wheels. "Road Kill" wheels a big Lexus. "Ice Pick" slams down the lane, running everyone else off it, in a gunmetal grey Hummer with a vanity license plate declaring: "UWANTSOMEOFME?" Extending his Nazi-possessions theme to the freeway, Bud has a big, black, blacked-out windows, chauffeur-driven Mercedes. No, it's more of a chauffeur-accompanied Mercedes, as the chauffer rides and Bud, incapable of relinquishing even steering wheel control, drives. I considered all these impressive statement-mobiles, but found myself giving my heart to another sensible Saaby. To be different. To be me, and that was something I didn't do very often. Even though I was as greedily rapacious as any of my cronies, I, for some reason, did not need a big shot car. I don't know why, I just didn't. And I felt good about that. It pleased me that my vehicle got good mileage and was low maintenance and that it was all the automobile I needed and nothing more. Something, perhaps the only thing that is unsullied about me, is represented by Saaby. I opened the door and slid into her cozy interior. I felt it, even standing still. That purity of spirit when I'm held safe and secure in her buttery, yet not top of the line, leather driver's seat. She knows me, so well.

The real me. How can I discard her? Saaby must be near me, always. Even when I'm with the Bhogwan, I shall ensconce her in secure, shaded, underground parking. She'll remain close at hand, a touchstone, proving, by her mere presence, that I wasn't that bad after all.

The following day Lynette and I are next to the barn.

"First you chip all the paint off. Then you sand the whole barn. Then you paint. One coat. Two coats. Three coats. Verstehen, senor?"

"I don't know how to paint."

"Then this'll be trade schoolin, too."

"Who's going to take the kids to school?"

"You. Paintin's in addition to."

"You can't make me do this."

"Seein as how we left things when you left, but didn't go, you might not want to p.o. me. Paint or sleep with the bobcats."

"You're getting back at me for yesterday. But you said things, too."

She treats this as if it weren't uttered.

"I'll be hittin the road tomorrow for Vancouver. Henrik'll answer any further barn makeover questions you may have."

She walks off. I call after.

"You can't stand that I've discovered the road to enlightenment. But I have and I'll get there, Lynette. Sooner or later I'll find my way to the Bhogwan Bhogwan and a sublimity you'll never know."

She turns around, continues walking, backwards.

"You seen CNN today?"

It's night. I'm in my cot, staring at Moose. Couldn't eat. Couldn't go in the kitchen. Too embarrassed. Humiliated. They indicted the Bhogwan. Money laundering, embezzlement. Fifty million stashed in the Cayman Islands. All these frizzed out people, tearfully telling America about the Bhogwan's mind control techniques. How he got them to sign over everything they had to him and then had sex with them while wearing fishnet hose, and then special guest Dr. Phil telling those dorks they have no self-esteem/worth/identity, which he addresses in his new book on sale everywhere, and then I ran out of the house thinking how could I have been so gullible. I'm not the sort of pathetic, desperate soul that falls for this magic cure crap. I don't buy dreams, I sell them. No, I don't. Not anymore. I'm the schmuck, now. That's how far I've fallen. Gone from con man to con-ee. After this, how can I trust any thought I have? What's the point? I mean, I've tried. No one can say I didn't try. I fought off my despair at losing my former life, heroically. I sought honesty, integrity. I was gutsy, tenacious and I've been mocked for it. That's how I feel. Ridiculed. Something, somewhere is having a giant guffaw at my expense. "Look at that idiot Paul. He keeps trying. Doesn't he know he can't win? Doesn't he know he's doomed? Hoo hoo hoo. Titter titter titter." Jesus. I feel so empty. I suppose I've always been empty, really. But at least before I had distractions. I could bury my head in the sand, or at least Lindsay. Now I'm just nothing. Unseen anti-matter. No one misses me. At work, everyone just gets to take one step forward. I'm sure "Pick" and "Kill" are scratching each other's eyes out for my office right now. Given Lindsay's attention span, it's likely she's forgotten I was ever in her life. Even Moose seems to be staring right through me. I am...*not,* anymore. And, if I don't really exist...may as well make it official.

In a storage cabinet, I find a folding chair.

A cliché is a great truth repeated so often its wisdom goes unheard. Take "you can't teach an old dog new tricks." Truly profound. Says it all, about how we become imprisoned by lifetime habits or beliefs. It is as sharply observed a comment on human nature as you will ever hear. If you hear it.

I find some rope.

Or, "The straw that broke the camel's back." Pure poetry and particularly apropos of my situation, if you substitute the left-right, body shot combination of "Bhogwan" and "ka-jarta" for "straw."

I tie one end of the rope into a loose knot and thread the other end through it. I toss the looped end over a big beam.

That small, additional frustration that tips the scales, far out of proportion to its own weight. You're in a boat, for example. It's taking on water. It takes on a ton. It still floats. It takes on another ton. It still floats. It takes on one more ounce. It sinks.

I loop the loop and yank it tight on the beam. I noose the other end.

So, for those of you who think it's preposterous to surrender because an elusive auto part prevented me from joining an ashram where I would be brainwashed and robbed blind, I ask that you view things from a larger perspective.

I open the folding chair. I stand on it.

Put it on Lynette's big screen. Because nothing is just what it is for me, these days. It's all more.

I ring the noose around my neck. I tighten it.

Or less.

I step off the chair.

"Mach aus! Mach schnell!"

My eyes flap open. I'm in my cot. Henrik's unshaven, road map face is millimeters from mine.

"Iss morgen. Vork now! Before iss hott!"

Holy hell, I'm alive. I must've fallen asleep before I could off myself. I buried my inconsolable disappointment at being un-hung in two-plus helpings of Henrik's sensationally sloppy biscuits and gravy breakfast. Now, hiccupping convulsively, I'm on a ladder and chipping barn paint. It's simple enough work. Scrape the paint with the tool, the paint peels off. Child's play. Boring but easy. Ten minutes later, as I'm not used to any domestic chore more physical than filling out a check to whomever is doing the job for me, I'm exhausted and only too happy to make my dual school run.

Then, back on the chain gang. In minutes my shoulders begin to burn. My arms. Before I get minimally less stupid and find some gloves, my fingers have a porcupine of splinters in them. I'm soon sweating, groaning. Lunch. More chipping. Ooh, my back. Is someone tying my spine in knots? It's so hot. It's a kiln. I stagger, sun-drunkenly, into the pickup. Scoop up Diana, who proclaims:

"Ew. You stink."

Drop her off at the house. Go get Eddie. Bring him home. Back's stiffer from driving. More chipping. Hunched over. Move the ladder. More chipping. Paint flecks in my eyes, in my sunburned ears. Dinner, at last. It's all I can do to raise a forkful of Henrik's mouthwateringly spectacular, sweet and sour-ish, Sauerbraten to my chapped and blistered lips. Barely able to hold my burnt eyelids open, I tote my blackberry pie back to the stall, where it sits, uneaten, for over twenty seconds and ten seconds after that, I comatose, narcolepse into a cryogenic state of unconsciousness so deep and dark I can't bring back my suicide dream, as hard as I try.

Next day. Still chipping. Somehow, I've managed to clean about half the barn but at the cost of total body mobility. I move with the agility of Herman Munster. When I lift my arms, they stay lifted. I'm something the dry cleaner over starched. But I don't care. I have nothing to look forward to. No future, just a permanent, miserable, now. Chipping's as good a way to spend it as any. Keeps me from hallucinating that there could ever be anything better.

Later, Henrik carries me into the house, fireman style, for Sloppy Joes and lemonade. After that, I seem to get a first wind. My muscles loosen to the extent that my shoulders no longer block my ears and then, without intending to, in chain gang, spiritual-style, I begin singing a Petty fave, "Learning to Fly."

And pretty soon, I'm chip-chipping with the beat of the tune. Smoothly. No gouging, no more clanking nails and temporarily numbing out an arm. So, I warble "The Waiting" and "Free Falling" and "Listen to Her Heart" and something, somewhere in the vicinity of my anus, frees up. Virility courses through my veins. I get carried away, do an air-guitar hip-kick thing during

"Refugee" which causes me to fly off the ladder and re-smash my nose, but even that can't stem the high tide of my hardy, workin man spirits. I swell with pride and labor on.

"Oooh...you wreck me, baby..."

I wail, while wallowing in the stench of my utterly male musk and, before I know it, Henrik's at the foot of the ladder and he's saying:

"Dat's enuff. You takin the vood."

And, damn, the whole barn is chipped. I hopscotch out and fetch Eddie, then Diana, who sneers:

"What're you so happy about?"

Sand. Paint. First coat. Second coat. Days later Henrik gushes:

"Dot's okay."

The sour kraut gives me more jobs. I do them. I hammer down a loose step. I un-stick a window by greasing its runners with lard. I mulch, spade, hoe, rake. I fear I've developed a tumor on my arm, then realize it's a burgeoning bicep muscle. I have enough energy, even after a rugged workday, for mid-afternoon diversions.

Lem says:

"This here's Luther. Luther, Mr. Paul."

I shake Luther's hand.

"Paul's my first name".

"A pleasure, Mr. Paul."

Luther's a Native American. He's 50, maybe. A visor clamped over his long, silver hair. A foot on the bumper of his new Range Rover, he's pulling on cowboy boots with soft-spikes in them. We're in the golf course parking lot. Lem's in knickers and her sheriff's hat. Rayno's in mechanic's overalls, filthy tennis shoes. He's knotted a kerchief on his hairless head and I'm stunned by how much he resembles a young Judi Dench.

Soldiers going into battle, we, in unison, sling our bags over our shoulders and head for the first tee.

"Hope our track ain't too tough on you, Mr. Paul."

"I'm a member at Briarcrest, Lem. Third highest slope in Southern California. I'm not too worried."

We round a corner and the course comes into view, below. Not what I'd expected. Set in a wooded hollow, you'd never know you were in the desert. Green as envy. Narrow, sweeping fairways. Tight doglegs that placed a premium on accuracy.

"Whoa. Sweet."

"Warnin. Don't come cheap. Kicked greens fees up to 12 bucks last month."

Rayno's on the tee, strangling his driver. His posture over the ball resembles a question mark. He aims left. Way left. Almost at the parking lot. He swings. The ball takes off. It slices. Banana slices. Boomerangs, almost. It ends up in the fairway, left of center.

"Dang. Not enough fade."

Luther steps up. He takes a moment and softly chants something. He then double-duck-hooks his drive left. He shrugs.

"Sometimes the answer is no."

Lem tees up. Wastes no time. Swings fluidly. Sets the ball out, right, with a tight draw. Two-forty, center cut.

"Nice shot, Lem."

"Thank you, sir. You know, we usually put a friendly wager on the game."

"Such as?"

"Skins. Straight up. Dime a hole. Carryovers."

"Good by me."

My turn. I pop a nice one, driving the dogleg on the left and gaining a good thirty yards on everyone.

"That'll play, Mr. Paul."

"Thanks, Lem."

I pick up my tee, feeling pretty satisfied.

"If you missed the water, round that bend."

"Water? There's water, there?"

They all grab their clubs. Begin walking.

"Nobody told me there was water."

＊

After the round, having co-colas and settling bets. I pay everyone. No one pays me. Rayno is regaling us with a tale of a recent confrontation with, he swears, a seven-toed cat. Lem and Luther are droll and witty skeptics:

"I think our boy's been hanging out with Jack Daniels again, Luther."

"Yeah. He musta been drunk."

Then, they pound the table and laugh really hard. Hurt and resentful, Rayno pierces them with an arrow from his verbal scabbard:

"One, two, three, four, five, six, seven. That's it. End a story."

Understandably pleased with himself, he chugs some

coke. Then, he runs a hand through his one hair. As he does, I offer:

"Rayno, can I ask you a personal question?"

"Baldness runs in the family."

"I didn't mean that."

"Grandma was bald, mama was bald…"

"It's your name. Rayno. It's very unusual."

"Oh. My given name's Raymond. But, when I was a pup, I's always getting into stuff. It's always, 'Ray no' this, 'n 'Ray no' that. Just stuck."

"I see."

"Beats on your self-esteem after a while, having 'no' as part of your name."

"Why don't you change your name?"

He chuckles, condescendingly.

"Then I just wouldn't know who I was, would I?"

I chuckle, too, at this Rubik's Cube logic. I turn to Luther and Lem, one of whom, I'm sure, will have the perfect acerbic retort to punctuate the moment. But, on this subject, Luther is solemnly nodding at Rayno. Lem, also. She offers:

"Change your name, change yourself."

"Forever," adds Luther.

That's nonsense. Or is it? What do I know? My name is changed, now. Inverted. Paul Quinlan became Quinlan Paul. Has it altered me? Am I evolving? If I am, common sense suggests it must be into something better. What I've been is just one of a million passengers on that fast track to nobody knows where. Running some 10K where, whenever you got to what should've been the end, there was a sign that said "more." So, you keep running, to the next sign, and the next and the next. No end. No *there*. Perhaps I'm zigzagging my way to a better place, now. Slaloming to something, who knows? Could be happening so slowly I'm not conscious of it. Hmm. Comforting thought. Thanks, Rayno, you've given me a new and much brighter perspective. I regard him fondly, as he yanks a long hair out of his nose. He scrapes the hair off his finger and into an ashtray. He bounces that same hair-finger off the table.

"I'm gonna find that cat, 'n then we'll all do some toe countin."

∗

I chop firewood. I unplug the garbage disposal, de-crud the gutters. I am the master of hyphenated chores.

A horn blares the first twelve notes of "Smoke on the Water." It's the triumphant return of Lynette. Eddie runs out to greet her. She shuts down her ground bound 767 and dismounts, like Chuck Yeager. Hugs Eddie.

"You been good?"

"Yeah."

"What about the promotion deal?"

"Working hard. Every night."

"That's my boy."

She spots the painted barn.

"Whoa!"

She sees me. I'm oiling the gravel.

"Nice barn job, Quinlan Paul."

"Piece of cake."

She steps up to me. Appraises.

"You're startin to look like a man whose body ain't just along for the ride."

"I'm sorry. My ears must be plugged. I thought I heard you compliment me."

"How're you feelin?"

The question startles me.

"What?"

She repeats her words, clearly enunciating them.

"How...er...you...feelin?"

"I'm feeling fine."

She clicks her teeth, then nods."

"Okay, then."

Eddie slides up to her.

"Get any tickets, ma?"

"Nope. Outran 'em again, honey."

She puts her arm around him. They walk toward the house.

"So...how's Diana?"

A very special welcome home dinner. Wiener schnitzel and spaetzle. Henrik even unscrewed a bottle of Mateus rosé for the occasion. Later, I masturbate so savagely that I bounce off the cot and have to consummate things on the floor. Not sure why I'm so tumescently aroused. The spaetzle?

*

Diana's in a cheerleader outfit today. Remarkably, my dislike of her has neutered all prurient thoughts.

"You're a cheerleader, huh?"

"Gee, how'd you figure that out?"

"Have you ever, in your entire life, uttered one word that wasn't sarcastic?"

"I'm not a cheerleader, yet, but I will be soon. The first of several tryouts is today."

"Break a leg. And I mean that."

"When I begin my acting career, having cheer led will bespeak well of my comfort in performing before others."

"That's a lot more noble than just, oh…rooting the team on."

She wearies of me and adjourns to admire her favorite person in the window.

"Lots of aspiring actresses in Los Angeles. I'd say you're prettier than some of them."

She sighs, as if to say that her belief in herself is far beyond undercutting. But then she blinks, too. She blinks twice.

∗

Eddie yawns.

"Tired, huh?"

"Studying late."

He yawns, again.

"I pass some test, they're gonna kick me up a grade."

"That'd be nice."

"Yeah. Like to be with kids more my own age, but this study material, it's hard, man."

"Oh, I'm sure you'll do fine."

He yawns, again. A little too long.

I glue down the bathroom linoleum. I bandini the vegetable garden. I straighten a fence post. I whistle while I work. I'm growing to love my undocumented alien toil. It's so fair. Labor equals results. What a wonderfully, non-manipulative way to spend one's days. It makes me feel…clean. Not physically clean, of course. I'm perpetually mucked and mired and so ripe I bring tears to my own eyes, but…spiritually fresh. Crisp. Like a brand-new room deodorizer. It's an exalting sensation. And I start to feel lucky…fortunate. So, I have some issues to deal with. Who doesn't? I've been a baby. A great big, whiny, feeling sorry for myself baby. Christ, Paul, you could have a disease. Cancer.

Leprosy. You could've been born with one of your eyes in your armpit. You're young, healthy. Your only problem is trying to figure out what to do with your life, and that, as things go, is hardly tragic. And, then it happens. As I joyfully pack down the ol' compost heap, I make a monumentally profound decision. I shall become a traveling, professional handyman. As flies dive-bomb and mosquitos Happy Hour on my legs, I compose my manifesto…to live simply and do good. I'll love myself for the altruistic choice I've made and become a totally fulfilled blue-collar being. Upon arrival in a charmingly gentrified hamlet, after checking into a quaint B&B and lunching at a regionally hip boîte, I'll cruise picturesque, tree-lined residential areas in Saaby, a sign in her rear window informing all: "Professional Handyman. Repairs and Odd Jobs While U Wait." Children will jump and shout and declare, "The handyman's here. The handyman's here." Thankful mothers will flag me down to unstop their clogged bathtubs or regrout their sinks. Every community will become a tad nicer for Johnny Handyseed having dropped by. I'll have a toolbox, of course. One of those neatly organized ones with sockets and duct tape and a level like Mr. Durning, the charming and beloved guy who lived across the street from Aunt Ina before the molestation charges. I'll carry lollipops, too, as he did, for the youngsters who gather, fascinated, as I practice my wizardry. I might even have a sucker or two for the occasional housewife whose husband is off working on an oil rig for six months. I'll awaken repressed rural sexuality, while sinking post holes. Yes, yes, I'll fix things. I'll fix the world. Eureka! I've found it. Oh…I need a cap. Got to have a cap. And on it I'll stencil these words, the most achingly beautiful words in the English language: "Paul The Handyman." This is it. This is what all my recent nuttiness has been leading to. Oh, hope, you're a fickle handmaiden. It's not irrelevant chaos. There is a purpose, in everything and I thank my stars I've found mine. Spooked, I jump two feet in the air.

"Eek! Shoo. Shoo, mouse."

*

"A handyman."

"Yep."

It's evening. Lynette and I are playing checkers on the coffee table/packing crate in the living room. Lynette shakes her head, raises one eye to engage both of mine and tell them the guy they're working for is an imbecile.

"Don't you see? This makes everything add up. There is a reason why my life fell apart and I ended up here, which was to discover my true vocation of handiness, so, even though I lost everything, I didn't lose anything at all because I found me."

"Call me a Silly Sally, but I thought you're here cause your car broke down."

"It has to be bigger than that. It has to be metaphorical. Metaphysical."

"Think I created me a Frankenstein."

"Meaning what?"

"Nothin."

"It's not nothing or you wouldn't have said it."

She lowers her eyes and manages to make that insulting, too. She moves a piece. The piece I wanted her to move. The piece that would lead her into my carefully laid trap.

"I put you workin to give that monkey mind of yours

a rest, but you're bound and determined to turn everything you do or don't do into craziness."

"You're saying you had me paint the barn as therapy?"

"Maybe."

"You're my psychiatrist, now?"

"Your move."

"That is so patronizing."

"Make a move, Quinlan, or I'm turnin on Aussie Rules Football."

"And now, the esteemed Dr. Lynette has decreed that I don't have the cojones to be a handyman. Thank you. Thank you so much for showing me the error of my ways."

"Yuppies ain't handymen."

"Oh? Have you noticed that your kitchen chair leg doesn't wobble anymore? Think it's a coincidence?"

"Putterin around the house's one thing. You try hirin yourself out, mark my words, tragedy will follow."

"Jesus Christ, Lynette. I'm lost, confused. Dust in the wind. I finally find some anchor and you ridicule it? Thanks a lot."

"Whyn't you get some other executive job? Do what you know?"

"Because doing what I know got me where I am. I have to do what I don't know a single thing about."

"Well, at least you're makin sense."

"I don't want to make sense. Sense made me miserable."

"And rich, as I recall."

"Money is nothing. A distraction, a panacea. Money makes you replace meaning with comfort."

"It'd make me replace the clothes dryer with one that worked."

"I have to kick the drug of materialism and find my place…the place I'm meant to be in. I'm on a journey. A quest. A modern-day Siddhartha."

"I don't know about him, but you ain't no damn handyman."

"Let me make that choice. I don't like being manipulated."

"Fine. Learn the dumb way. And make your move."

"Oh, I'm going to make my move. And when I do, Lynette…this strategically set-up masterpiece of a move, you will see that my mind is working just fine. That it's a steel trap and more than capable of leading me to wise and judicious life choices."

I slide my piece up a square. In a flash, she grabs one of her checkers and hop-hops over five of my pieces, ending up on the back line.

"King me, Sid."

*

Lem and I stare at a clump of six-foot reeds that appear to have a red ball cap atop them.

Whoosh.

The reeds ruffle. Rayno's voice rings out.

"That's eight."

Lem offers:

"Rayno, you're gonna get chiggers. Take your penalty and drop it outta there."

The ball cap emerges from the weeds. With Rayno under it.

"She's settin up, this time. I can wedge it."

He bounces his club into the bag, wrestles a rusted pitching wedge out and pushes back into the bush, a big game hunter, hot on the trail of triple bogies. As he goes, he utters over his shoulder:

"Mr. Paul. Heard some place in Dubuque had a Ka-jarta. Called em yesterday."

"Rayno, that's wonderful. When can you get it?"

The bush seems to speak:

"Can't. False alarm. Just wanted you to know, I'm still on it."

"Yes, I can see how hard you're working, right now."

Whoosh.

"Shoot. Nine."

Lem sets her golf bag on the ground. Two metal legs spring out to hold it upright.

"We might be here a spell."

She flips up a seat that's attached to the bag. She plops.

"Did someone drop him on his head as a child?"

"Twice, I hear. So, were you tellin Luther you're a handyman, now?"

"Yes. Yes."

I step to her.

"I am *Paul the Handyman*."

Whoosh.

"Ten."

"I got a leakin septic line they want arm 'n a foot to

fix. You reasonable?"

"I'd have to double my rates to be dirt cheap."

"Hmm. I'll think on it.

My god. A potential customer. It begins.

Whoosh.

"That don't count. I was killin a snake."

*

"So, how're the cheerleader tryouts going?"

"Yeah, you care."

"C'mon. You can't pass up an opportunity to talk about yourself."

She snorts. One second. Two seconds.

"The finals are next Tuesday. I'm very confident."

"Good."

She cranks my rearview mirror so it's facing her and begins brushing her hair.

"They all have surgery, you know."

"Who does?"

"Those pretty young actresses. I could too, if necessary."

"Really? Can they un-thicken ankles, now?"

"Fuck you! Fuck you, twice!"

I laugh.

*

"Did you go to college?"

"Yes, I did, Eddie."

"Oh."

He drums his hands on his knees.

"This test…sure gonna be hard."

I say nothing.

*

"Detergent."

I reach for a giant box.

"No, no. The big one."

She points to another container. One a family of six could live in and have room for a den.

"You got a lot to learn about bein poor. Check the sticker."

She points to a tiny sign underneath the soap.

"Point-five cents cheaper per ounce. Two free washes a year."

"Good. That'll pay for my truss."

I attempt to haul the big bruiser off the shelf. Surprisingly, I do. Wow. I'm a stud now. Yes, we're at the Big Mart. Lynette, The Frugal Trucker, is giving me a crash course in skinflinting. We move up the aisle, she checking her list. Remarkably, she has no trouble with Henrik's handwriting.

"I want to hit the tool aisle before we go. Price some hammers."

"For the last time, Quinlan, leave Lem's septic tank to a pro."

"I am a pro. And…"

Her head jerks like a roped calf. She waves a silencing hand at me. Her nostrils flare. The nose goes left, right, radar tracking. It zeroes in on:

"Pupus."

She spins, sniffs her way up the aisle. I follow.

"You think this is a whim, don't you? A lark. It isn't. I'm spending two hours every night at the 'So, You Want to be A Handyman' web site. So, there."

But she's on a mission. We come to a Chinese

woman at a stand. She offers two mini-mini-cups of gooey dough in her plastic gloved hand.

"Can I interest you in some Ploger's Almond Roll?"

"Is a bear a Catholic?"

Lynette snatches both the cups.

"How about you, sir? They're delicious."

"Chow down, Q.P."

I reluctantly accept one. We sample the samples. Surprisingly, it's gooey dough.

"Umm. This shit's great."

She grabs another sample.

"So, how's Eddie been?"

"Fine, I guess."

"He's tryin to get moved up a grade."

"So, I've heard."

"Ain't easy. You know any real bright, probably college educated people, could help him out?"

"Why is everybody, and not very subtly, trying to turn me into a tutor?"

"No man stands taller'n when he stoops to help a child."

She slips another sample into a pocket.

"I'm not getting involved. My car could be ready any

time, and forty seconds after it is, I will be gone and beginning my new career."

"You ain't no handyman."

"I ain't no schoolmarm, neither."

"Fair enough. We'll leave it now that you're thinkin about it."

"I said…"

"U-turn this aisle. Forgot 409."

I attempt to swing the Army tank-sized shopping cart around without asphalting the floor with innocent shoppers.

"Is today Tuesday?"

"All day."

"Tryout day."

"What's that?"

"You know. Diana's finals for cheerleader."

"What?"

"She didn't tell you?"

But Lynette's halfway down the aisle.

"Lynette? Hey."

She skids round the corner and disappears.

*

"Gonna beat you, gonna eat you up…ain't no lie. Tell your friends your butt's been whupped by Brigham High. Yay!"

The blond girl jumps as high as her pigmentation permits.

I caught Lynette in the parking lot. She would've taken off solo, but I had the keys. She almost took a finger as she wrested them from my grasp, and I'd barely scrambled into the passenger side when we were off on another retro-rocket ride either from or to hell. She took a shortcut, which meant, as we were shearing down the highway, she, suddenly and without warning, violently inverted the steering wheel 120 degrees and, as I attempted to pry my inertia-challenged face from the passenger's window, we began hydroplaning directly across the desert floor. I coughed up one and a half kidneys as we caromed through, around and over gullies, hoots and hollers on our own Paris to Dakar to the mortuary rally. Barrancas. Culverts. Chicane. Bighorn sheep bleated unheeded warnings as on and up and sideways we careened. Lynette was muttering. I was desperately trying to re-attach my suddenly severed seat belt buckle. Then, it appeared. The cliff ledge. We vaulted over it and, after remaining aloft so long I had time to both pass out and re-awaken, we banged down onto the Brigham School driveway on one wheel. We rumbled up it on two and just as I'd wrenched my head out of the roof lining it was jerked violently sideways, stopping one inch from the windshield as the tumbleweed infested, gopher-in-the-grill pickup came to an abrupt, smoking tire ceasefire, two inches from a new Rolls Royce. The Duchess of Hazard was sprinting for the big building before the student we'd almost hit had climbed back out of the bushes. After gently prodding my skull back into a position generally facing forward, so when I vomited, which I then did, I wouldn't have chunks on my back, I staggeringly followed her into the gym and now we're in a corner, viewing the nubile proceedings. The cheerleader leader is a 40-year-old bottle of vanilla with a page boy hairdo and a whistle around her neck.

"That was very nice, Cyndy, but you spin and pivot after 'Eat you up.' You forgot the pivot."

"Shit! May I try it again, Ms. Howley? Please?"

"You did try it, Cyndy. That's why it's called a tryout."

Lynette, arms planked across her chest, is studying Diana who's planted in the front row of bleachers, arms pinning her chest. Now, Cyndy approaches Ms. Howley.

"Please, Ms. Howley. One more try. I know I can please you."

Cyndy strokes Ms. Howley's shoulder as she pleads. Ms. Howley enjoys this. Cyndy knows she enjoys this.

"What the heck. You go, girl."

Cyndy re-routines. Diana sneers. Then, her two eyes and mouth simultaneously spring open as wide as possible. She's spotted us. As Cyndy spins and pivots, Diana slinks over to us.

"What are you doing here?"

"Come to offer emotional support, darlin."

"Support?"

That said, fearfully:

"Honey, I'm your mother and I care, I truly do, about the important chapters in your life, of which this is surely one."

"Mother…"

"I know I ain't always been there, or if I was, I been passed out and wasted most the time, but it's a new day.

"Diana Clark."

Diana pirouettes.

"Coming, Ms. Howley."

She spins back to us.

"Leave!"

Spins back again. Smiles. She bounds, pompoms pompoming. She's very athletic. High jumps, tight twirls but, to me, she's clearly distracted by Lynette's presence. She falls. Spectacularly. Head over ass over elbow. Sprawled on the floor, she pounds it, as her fellow competitors howl. Lynette runs up to her.

"It's okay, sweetie. Anyone can fall. I saw Mary Lou Retton fall once."

Diana stares at her mother, mortified, as a buzz comes up among the other girls.

"Samantha Collins."

Lynette turns to Ms. Howley.

"What?"

"Next girl, please."

Samantha steps up. Lynette body checks her away, then approaches Ms. Howley.

"Ain't you gonna give Diana another chance?"

"Who are you?"

129

"Her mother."

Diana groans.

"The concert pianist?"

"Huh?"

Giggles. Diana emits a dolphin wail, jumps up and runs out of the room.

"I mean...I sorta retired from the ivories. Fingers was getting short. But you gave that Cyndy girl a second chance. You should give Diana one, too."

"I don't have to justify myself to you."

"You're supposed to be fair, ain't you?"

"I am fair. I'm also qualified in this area and you are not."

"Oh, yeah?"

Lynette flips. Literally. She does a standing still back flip. She cartwheels across the floor, her body a blur, in a perfect circle around the perimeter of the room. She sticks a perfect landing, right back at the feet of Ms. Howley.

"Do that, soul sister."

"I think you should leave."

"Look, lady..."

"Cartwheel right on out that door, before I call Security."

Lynette leans into Ms. Howley.

"Maybe Diana just ain't playin the game, huh? Maybe she ain't battin her eyes at you in the come hump me manner of that whore, Cyndy, there, that seemed to get your grease all sizzlin."

Ms. Howley gasps. The girls gasp. I jump up and down, happily.

"Maybe I'll be havin a sit down with the Principal. Maybe I'll be callin some of my fellow parents. Maybe I'll be droppin by the goddam *High Desert Times*. Maybe I'll be faxin the fuckin 'O'Reilly Factor'! Or..."

Lynette hones in, even closer to Ms. Howley. Their faces are close enough to be kissing.

"...Maybe you'll be givin my Diana, who's so talented and worked so hard, the second chance it's only human decency to give."

Ms. Howley slides her face away from Lynette's. She's pretty shook up. Not so shook up that when their mutual breasts touched an electrical charge didn't shoot through her that could power Sao Paolo for a week, but still shook up.

"Perhaps I was rash. Tell Diana she can try, again."

Lynette smiles.

"I knew you was good people."

Diana's marching down the long driveway. Pulling the pickup alongside her, Lynette leans out her window.

"You got another chance."

Head forward, Diana keeps moving. Lynette rolls the truck along with her.

"You get to try your routine again."

"I heard you."

She keeps walking.

"So you fell. Can't let that get you. You gotta fight for what you want, honey."

"How could you? How could you humiliate me, like that?"

"I was standing up for you, Diana."

"Too little, too late, mom."

"C'mon. Get in the car."

"I'll walk."

"It's 20 miles."

Diana stops walking. Lynette stops the truck.

"I'll get in, but only if you promise to keep away from me...to leave me alone...to mind your own damn business."

"I do. I promise that. One hundred percent."

She raises a hand, as if making a Girl Scout pledge. Diana twitches her mouth.

"I hate you, you know."

She comes around to my side. I open the door and get out to let her in.

"I'm not sitting next to her."

I climb back in the truck, slide over to the middle. Diana gets in and closes the door. Lynette pulls out, slowly. We drive the speed limit all the way home, with nary a word uttered.

*

"I told you...no wire HANGERS!"

On the TV, Joan Crawford pummels her daughter while wearing ghoulish white stuff on her face. Lynette, slumped on the sofa, observes morosely. I'm next to the couch, having just come in from the kitchen.

"Uh, Lynette. Supper's ready."

She mutes the TV. She ponders. She stands. She mechanically walks out the door. Moments later, I hear the pickup's engine and seconds later tire gravel peppers the front window.

＊

In the morning, Lynette's still AWOL. When Eddie wonders where she is, I tell him I saw her go off early for some car parts. No point flipping the kid out. It's Saturday, so I don't need the pickup for school duty, but when it's afternoon and she's not back, I'm about to tell him the truth. He might want to get Lem in on this. Then, I hear tires. I go out front. Lem and Lynette are getting out of Lem's Nissan pickup with a siren on top. Lynette's all thrashed. Hair frizzed. T-shirt torn. Bruises on her arm and face. She moves toward the house, head down. Lem hustles up and grabs her arm.

"You pay damages, I'll try to get the charges dropped. But friendship only goes so far, Lynette. You get bar brawlin again, I'm lockin you down."

Lynette nods. Lem releases her arm. Lynette brushes past me and goes into the house. Lem, hands on her hips, shakes her head.

"She beer mugged some guy who artificially inseminates cows."

"Probably something Freudian, there. She had a run in with Diana, yesterday."

"We all got issues, Quinlan. If Lynette wants to beat herself up, she should punch out her own lights and eliminate the middle-man."

"I agree."

"Then tell her that, when you talk to her."

"Pardon me?"

"About getting her dang ducks in a row."

"I'm not talking to her about ducks, or anything else."

"Quinlan, if you're gonna live with people, you gotta get involved."

"I'm not living here. I'm waiting to leave."

"So, you're gonna sit on the sidelines, even though a bright guy like you's probably got a ton of balm to offer that painfully, desperate woman? Not lift a finger to lessen another human's abject misery of constant sorrow? If that don't churn your colon, fine. Not my way to pressure you."

"Oh, that's good, Lem. Very slick. If you ever want

to get into sales, I've got a number for you in L.A."

She turns to her car, opens the door.

"Tee time's changed to nine-fifteen tomorrow."

She plops onto the seat.

"Less Lynette's still too distraught for you to leave."

She pops the car in gear and slowly drives away.

*

I hike up the rock. Lynette's there, sitting Indian-style and smoking. If she hears me coming, she's not letting on, just staring out at the flame red sky. I mosey over to the edge.

"You sure do get some sunsets, around here."

"I'm havin a private time, Quinlan. Beat it."

I have no idea what to say. I pretend I'm a character on a soap opera.

"You've hidden out all day, Lynette. I know you're in pain. Maybe it would help to talk."

"You sound like a soap opera."

"I'm here. If you have nothing to say, I'll leave."

"Nothin to say."

"I tried."

I'm about to turn away.

"Except, I'm a rotten mother and my kid hates me."

Great. Now, I have to respond. I open my mouth, and out comes:

"And you'll improve that by reverting to your old ways?"

"Shit. You see right through me."

I do?

She stubs out her smoke.

"I gotta keep it together. Fight for my family, right?"

"From what I've observed, you're building a new life. A better one. Diana'll see that, if you just keep it up."

"Hmm."

"Or maybe she won't. But what other choice do you have?"

She lights another cigarette.

"Gonna pout a spell more, Quinlan."

"Then, I'll be off."

I turn to go.

"But I heard you."

Said to my back. Amazing what you can come up with when you're not trying.

*

"How come you're such a bitch?"

I can't help myself. This brat is getting to me.

"I don't know. Why?"

She says it while preening, as usual, in the window.

"That school costs a fortune. Are you paying for it?"

"She owes me more than that."

"Nobody owes anybody anything."

"You have no idea how it's been. Her men, her drugs. Leaving us a few dollars and disappearing for days. And she's still doing it, now."

"This time you drove her to that, Diana."

"All she's cared about is herself. Ever. And I should feel bad because now she's guilty? Let her suffer all the rest of her goddam, useless life because I'm going to spend the rest of mine trying to overcome what she's done to me."

"At least you have a parent, Diana. Some of us never did."

"I don't want to talk about this, anymore."

"Fine. Because I don't want to talk to you."

We drive in silence for several minutes. I work on a way to play this snot.

"I was kidding the other day. You're certainly attractive enough to be an actress."

No response.

"It's so competitive, though. You need state of the art training."

She studies her shoes.

"The University of Southern California has an excellent drama school. Expensive, of course. Big, big bucks. You got the grades for a scholarship?"

It takes a few seconds.

"Probably not."

"Well, the mother you want to tar and feather would probably hock her rig for 20 years to pay the tuition…if you'd just throw her a damn bone."

I glance over. She's mulling. First rule in selling is, get them to mull. Then, let them decide to do what you want them to do.

"Yep. Showing up for dinner, once in a while, could pay some very healthy dividends."

Two minutes til supper. Meatloaf, mashed potatoes and corn on the cob. Date pudding for dessert. I'm seated, napkin tucked into my shirt, knife and fork locked and loaded, salivary glands on overdrive. Lynette, who's been scarce all day, enters the kitchen with a kick in her stride.

"Somethin smells like roses you could eat."

Her sass is back. She's got a weak chin, but she does keep getting up. She moves to the stove. Prepares to serve the food.

"Eddie, how's your studying goin?"

"Pretty good."

"What's the capital of South Dakota?"

"It's, uh…I don't know, mom."

I have a hunch he does. I do, too. It's Minot.

"It's Pierre. Pierre, South Dakota."

I meant Pierre.

"Remember it. Could be on your test. Henrik, grab that other plate."

She hauls two heaping plates to the table. Henrik follows with the other.

"What you could use is a Brain Coach for your test, that means so much to your future. Course, we ain't got nobody that high I.Q around here."

She gives me half an eye, as she sets the plates down.

I'm about to take my first bite when Diana walks in. She steps to the always empty chair and sits. Everyone reacts. Even Henrik coughs and smacks at a fly on his face. Diana announces:

"I'm just eating. Nothing more."

Silence. I could say something, of course. I could say it was my sly and psychologically astute machinations that brought about this watershed mother-daughter détente in the making. But that would be self-serving and not in the spirit of the moment. So, I just think it.

"Your hair's nice."

"Thank you, Eddie."

Lynette, doing a lot of blinking, coughs into her napkin. Then stands.

"Guess we'll be needin another plate."

She goes to get it.

*

I'm driving Eddie to school.

Beeeeeppp.

"Angh!"

I jump. My beeper! Bud's found me! I knew it! No one can hide from him. Why did I even try? Who do I think I…hold on…I don't have a beeper anymore. Oh, it's Eddie's. He's reading the message.

"Step on it."

"What is it?"

"Go past the church. One mile, then right."

"What about school?"

"Stand on it!"

I do.

Rafe's Place is a cool and dark cave, after the sun. When my eyes adjust I see, as it's eight-thirty in the morning, no one's around except the bartender. Oh, and this porky guy, in a cheap suit and bolo tie, who's sitting on a stool. He's got a shot of something in front of him and he's staring at it. Eddie slides onto the stool next to fatso. He nods at the server.

"Thanks for calling, Red."

"Next time mind your own business, Red," offers chubs.

I sit down next to Eddie.

"Drink it, Cozy."

"I'm gonna."

"Drink it now. Or I will."

"Don't be cute, kid."

Eddie lifts the drink to his lips. Cozy grabs his drinking arm.

"You got two good years, asshole."

"And you've got 46 good days."

Cozy takes the drink from Eddie. They eye-to-eye. Cozy pushes the glass away.

"I can't work. I can't think anymore."

"Yeah, you can."

"My encouragement died."

He points to the drink.

"Not drinking's the easy part, Coze. Living's the hard thing."

"That's some true shit, brother."

"Besides, working for the government isn't a real job, anyway. You forget how to shuffle papers and drink coffee?"

Cozy smiles. He ruffles Eddie's hair.

"You're a good sponsor."

He motions to Red.

"Coupla ginger ales."

Eddie turns to me.

"Want a ginger ale?"

"Tell you what. I'll buy."

*

After dinner, I climb up on the rock where Eddie's studying. I help him for a couple of hours.

I replace four light bulbs and a fuse. Oh, Diana said something at dinner. I help Eddie the next night. And the night after that. Diana allows Lynette to attend her first cheerleading game, with the proviso she not tell anyone who she is.

*

"You sure you're up to this?"

"Of course."

I'm with Lem, trying not to vomit as we're directly over the septic leak.

"Nothin's cheap, Quinlan, if it ain't done right."

Buyer's remorse. Seen it 100 times.

"Lem, Lem, Lem…"

I reassuringly hitch up my handyman belt, which has lots of shiny new tools hanging from it.

"This is…ach!"

A slight awl-puncturing-scrotum problem. I re-shift the belt.

"This is…what I do."

"Guess everybody's gotta start somewhere."

"You won't be sorry. I promise."

It wasn't my fault. Was not. The problem was the instructions from the "Septic Strategy" web page. I didn't discern this until long after the event…but the section that said, "WARNING: Excavating down to the leak, can release the only restraint to its virtual explosion. Engage cut off valve first," came not before but *after* the paragraph that said, "Excavate down to the leak." The literal upshot of this shoddy, and possibly class-action lawsuit, technical writing was a 40-foot poopgeyser. It showered me, Lem and her cat, "Kitty," who, since that day, clucks like a chicken and dives under the bed every time the toilet flushes. Henry Hank, the plumber I had to call, informed me:

"You're supposed to engage the cut off valve, first."

And then:

"Keep fixin pipes. I wanna retire, early."

Then, he belly-laughed and billed me 850 dollars to bring that happy day a mite closer. Luckily, Lem consented to not tell Lynette about the doody debacle in return for my pledge to sell my tools and never handyman again.

Am I bitter? In a word, yes. I truly thought I'd found that place of contentment life had reserved for me. Now having doubts as to whether such residence exists. I'm drifting at present. Sleeping late. Eating way too much. I don't know. Perhaps the handyman business was just a test. To see if I had the real goods before fate will bathe me in the cosmic light of self-understanding. If that's so, I'm getting a failing grade. In fact, I'm not bitter. That would suggest an energy level I don't presently possess. I'm just here, right now. Taking up space. Watching Spanish Language TV a lot. That I don't understand a word being spoken seems somehow appropriate.

*

"This is not what I do, Lynette."

"What you do is nothin, all day, which is about to change."

We're at "The Stand." Some falling-down stand up at the highway. Apparently, Lynette is also a date farmer. Or rancher. They must have some trees, somewhere. Or bushes, or whatever the hell dates grow on, because Lynette, cigarette pasted to lip, is unloading a scale, plastic bags and boxes and boxes of sticky, smelly dates, which it is now, I've been informed, my duty to spend each simmering, sweltering, griddle-cake day, offering up to lost RV-ers and crazed serial killers taking a break for dried fruit.

"Ah, another emotional kick start from the cowgirl shrink?"

"I want you out here dawn to dusk, weekends included."

"I'll be bored to tears."

"Not so. We get good drive-by since A-40 flash flooded. But if you need entertainment…"

She slaps a radio Fred Flintstone used on the counter.

"Clear day, you can get Gallup."

She heads for her truck.

"Don't leave me here."

She gets in the pickup. Juts her head out.

"When you're weighen those dates, don't mind if your thumb takes a rest on the scale. Customers 'spect you to."

And, vroom, she's gone. Something flies by, really low. A buzzard? Was that a buzzard?

*

"How bout a date?"

He guffaws, in flawless imitation of the Disney character "Goofy."

"That's very funny, Rayno."

It's been three interminable, dust-munching days. This is my first customer of the fourth. I pop open a sack.

"How much do you want?"

"Eight."

"Eight pounds?"

"Eight dates."

I count out the dates.

"Where's your tip jar?"

"I don't have a tip jar.

I hand him his dates.

"Seventy cents."

He hands me a dollar. I give him change. He slips the quarter into my shirt pocket. Keeps the nickel.

"'Preciate your helpful service, anyway."

"Thank you. I'll put it into a T-Bill. Any luck with the ka-jarta?"

"Lots. All bad. Date?"

He offers his date bag.

"I think I have all the dates I need, Rayno."

"Oh. Right."

"Look, when you talk to people about the car part, suggest, if they find it, there might be something extra in it for them."

"Extra, what?"

"Money. A reward."

"Oh. Uppin the ante, huh?"

"It's been a month, Rayno."

"Really? Tempus fugits."

He munches a date, thoughtfully, if such a term can be applied to Rayno.

"Maybe I shouldn'ta sent that ka-jarta back."

"What ka-jarta?"

"Hmm?"

"You said you shouldn't have sent the ka-jarta back."

"I did?"

"Yeah. You did."

He blushes. Swallows his date.

"I gotta go."

He hurries for his rusted Subaru station wagon. I'm

over the counter and on him like spandex on a sumo wrestler.

"What was the first ka-jarta, Rayno?"

"I gotta get to my dental bleachin."

He opens the car door. I reach in and rip the keys from the ignition.

"If you don't tell me, and this minute, your keys are desert bound and your teeth will be yellow, forever."

"No, sir. No, way. I ain't no stoolie."

He paces in anguish. I raise my arm to throw.

"Talk or walk, Rayno!"

He blubbers:

"I got the ka-jarta. Way back when. Phoenix had one. Put it in your Sabe, ready to go. Lynette called and said you'd went insane loony bonkers and was goin to see some Hog Man, who'd rip off all your money and brainwash your brain and that I should make like I couldn't fix your car so I took the ka-jarta back out cause I had a cousin who was in one a them cults in Mexico and they made her cut off her pinky toe and ever since, she falls down a lot and that's what I was rememberin at the time, as I tried to save you from yourself, but it wasn't really my idea."

It takes me a week to respond.

"You sent the ka-jarta back."

"All our hearts was in the right place, Mr. Paul."

"They've sold it, by now, of course. The only one in, perhaps, the whole country."

"But you still got your pinky toe."

I step close to him and give him the badass eye.

"The game's over now, Rayno. You're going to fix my car. You're going to find that part, right?"

"Yessir."

"I'm from L.A. We don't get what we want, we start shooting people, you hear me?"

"Loud and clear, sir."

He does everything but salute.

"All right."

I hand him his keys and say, nicely:

"Could you drop me off at Lynette's on your way?"

*

"I saved your sorry ass, is what I did."

"No. You deprived me of the moral and ethical right to make my own decisions."

"Where's my lighter?"

She's not trying to find her lighter. She's running from room to room to get away from me and I'm not letting her.

"I'm outraged, Lynette. Livid. You're not my parent. I'm a responsible, capable adult."

"A-huh. That's why Lem's cat thinks it's a chicken."

"What? Did she tell you about that?"

"Henry Hank. He was buyin everybody drinks on you. Thanks for the Rum Collins, plumber boy."

She's out of the kitchen. Me, too. The swinging door smashes my nose, but deters me not.

"The issue is not whether or not my decisions are wise. The issue is, do you have the right to intercede, which you don't."

"The issue is, where's my damn Bic?"

She clomps down the hallway. I'm her shadow.

"No one who's made as many wrong turns as you is qualified to show me the correct way to do anything."

"I'm merely self-destructive, Quinlan. You're psycho."

She ducks into her bedroom. I follow.

"I'm searching. I'm on the path to a better me. I demand the right to take it."

She stops, turns on me. We bump foreheads.

"Wasn't for me, you'd be shave-headed, chantin up people in airports and callin yourself 'Rama Dong' by now. You should be thankin me for steppin in when I didn't have to. In fact…now I'm gettin pissed…I want a 'Thank you very much, Lynette,' right this minute."

"Dream on, Miss Run-Away-Whenever-The-Going-Gets-Tough."

"Bite me, Mr. Gushin-Septic-Shitstain."

"I hate you."

"I hate you more."

"Bitch!"

"Yuppie prick!"

"Bitch bitch!"

"Get outta my goddamn face!"

"Make me, bitch."

We stand, frozen, for a moment. Then, we kiss. Pugilistically. We bite. We nibble. We chew. We wet-sand each other's necks with our tongues. We're on the bed. We thrash and groan and rip and bong our heads together. We slash each other's clothes off. We're inside out, upside down. I gnaw her toes, screw her armpit. She sucks my finger. I harmonica her tits. She

153

spanks me. I lick grease from her fingernails as she chews my eyebrows. We hump so hard we make butter. I give her an NFL running back caliber fake-and-thrust. Her eyes roll back in her head. My tongue iguana flicks her ear. She's on top. I'm on top. Side-side. I airplane propeller her.

"Yanga!"

"Yanga dun!"

"Animawa!"

When I awake, I'm alone. Did what happened, really happen? I'm in her bed, well…on her mattress, which is now half onto the floor. There's a ribbon of nail scratches on the wall. A lampshade's on my foot. I have a hickey on my right testicle, so, I guess it did. Wow. Where did that come from? And was I a beast, or what? This encounter made my trysts with Lindsay seem positively Amish. I never knew I possessed such passion. Will we do it, again? Oh, I hope, I hope. Gotta give my little buddy some recovery time, though. Right now it's an English banger without the casing. Man. I'm thrashed. Can't move. Maybe some more rest. Feels so good. Post-poking languor. Who knew I was such a pony-stud? Oh…this is so nice. Lying on a real mattress. So soft, yet not too soft. Really whipped. Really, really…

"Mmm."

I pass out.

*

When his people had a problem they couldn't crack, Thomas Edison used to have them all take a nap. "When we wake, we will have our answer," he'd advise. It was uncanny, how true that often was. I suppose it has something to do with letting go of preconceived notions…freeing the imagination…allowing new thoughts to enter the picture. That's how it was with me, anyway. I arose from my slumber feeling…I'm not sure how to describe it. I just sensed that something was in the air. Some revelatory thought, and all I had to do was grab it. Then, it came to me, so clearly…it was so obvious, that I had to laugh. Of course, of course. It's so simple…so *right*. I mean, I'm not one to pound my own pud, but it's now plainly apparent that I'm the hottest hump-monkey who ever drew breath. That's why I'm going to be a porn star, when I leave here. That's right. Don't laugh. I'm serious. My twelve round booty bob with L proved beyond any doubt that I am light years beyond the amateur ranks of screwing. I have a gift. I'm a late blooming wunder-fuckin-kind and it would be almost criminal to not demonstrate, to video renting wankers everywhere, the steamy red-hot chili pepper moves I've mastered that would turn even their chaste, librarian girlfriends into pecker-grabbing-under-the-restaurant table, living-to-hump, slutty bitch tramps. Yes, yes, this is it. This is my vocation. My true calling of the wild. I'm a rebel, a social outlaw. Off the grid, under the radar, pushing the envelope. Living on the fringes of the shadows…shedding the shackles of an uptight, hypocritical society. Making my own rules. Ooh, ooh. I've even got my name picked out. It's…

"Haw haw haw haw haw."

I just told Lynette my porn name.

"Dick Tater! Haw haw haw haw haw."

"It's a good name. Evocative."

"Please. My liver's bouncin."

We're in the kitchen. Out of breath, she sits on her chair. Damn, it's wobbling again. She wipes her eyes on her shirtsleeve.

"Quinlan, you're as all over the place as anyone I ever knew who wasn't sniffin gas tanks."

"That's the point. I've explained all this to you. I need to be grounded. I need a new identity. Some self-respect."

"Well, porn-starrin is right below bein Pope on the most admired list."

"It's an inspired idea and I want your promise you will not interfere."

Her body language says she's about to respond negatively, but she stops herself. Her eyes internalize for a second, and she says:

"Fine."

"I mean it, Lynette. You play with my plans, again, I will never forgive you. Never, ever. Do you hear me?"

"I said fine. It's your dream, even if it's wet."

"Thank you. And, as I'll be embarking on my new adventure, shortly, you must guard against becoming too smitten with me."

"Smitten?"

"It would be very understandable."

"Kinda full of yourself, ain't you?"

"Technically speaking, it was you who was full of me.

And moaning quite appreciatively, as I remember."

"Yeah, well per that, I am off men for life plus 20 years. That last tango was just that. One a them stress-reducin, one-time things."

"Oh, I wasn't suggesting we can't have sex, again."

"No, I suggested that, so don't go weenie-waggin around me no more"

"But I need to practice my hot guy moves for what I suspect will be a grueling and stress-filled porn audition."

"Then you better get you a blow-up woman. Now, I gotta scoot. Me and Diana are off to Kellum for *A Day of Health and Beauty*."

She stands.

"We been hittin it off pretty good lately, surprise, surprise."

"Well, she's a loving human being, with absolutely no ulterior motive."

"So, where you plan to go, to make your stiffy a household name?"

"Maybe San Francisco."

"Good bread. Freeways bottleneck, too much. Later, Dick Tater."

"Later, Lynette."

She pushes open the door and leaves.

*

Lynette trucks for Baton Rouge. The cheerleader leader, Ms. Howley, runs off with a female biker. Lynette returns for one night, then heads off to Scranton. Rayno has a hole-in-one, the ball caroming off an occupied restroom onto the green 30 yards away and into the cup, but doesn't find a ka-jarta. Lynette returns again, this time for a week. I borrow her truck and head on over to Hollis. A quick 80-mile jaunt, where, at an establishment named Hi-Life Adult Video and News Store, my research has revealed open male porn auditions are to take place. As I enter a room that seems to be the establishments office, I see six or seven fairly normal-looking men. I find a chair as a pudgy older fellow enters, enthusiastically clapping hands. He says: "Hey guys, I'm Ernie to those who don't know me. So, good to see ya. Let's get to 'er. Stand, drop trou...you know the deal." We all stand, lower our pants and shorts. For some reason the guy next to me

159

starts giggling. Then another. Soon everybody except me is laughing, including Ernie. And they're all looking at me. At my groin.

Okay. Let me make this clear, because I checked. A five-and-a-half-inch long penis is exactly in the middle of normal size. I'm not the freak. Those laughing fools inside are. They're the weirdos. They're the freaks. Probably have to store their dicks with one of those hose roller things. Who the hell needs that? Not me, buddy. Not me one bit! I never even wanted to be a stupid porn star. I never said that. I said horn star! Yeah., that's it. I'd like to play the sax!

"Where'd they get the train?"

"Pardon?"

"For the Underground Railway?

"There was no train, Eddie. That's a euphemism for the network of people who helped the slaves get to the north."

"What's a euphemism?"

We're on the rock. Been pushing hard, as the test is just a few days away. Eddie seems overloaded.

"I'll tell you tomorrow. Let's wrap it up."

"It's early."

"We'll make up for it."

"Okay."

He closes his book. I like this kid.

"Eddie, I'm, uh…glad you're okay, now."

"Me, too."

He sits there.

"I used to feel so alone. Then I found out people will help you if you let them."

"Mmm."

He stands.

"So, think your car'll be ready before I have the test?"

"I don't know."

"It'd be cool to share it with you, if I pass."

"I'll stick around, til the big day."

"Yeah? That's great."

"Go to sleep."

"Right. Good-night, Paul."

"Night, Eddie."

He moves off. I yawn. I look up. A hundred thousand million stars. Such a big world. Makes me shiver.

*

"I'm going to buy my mother a birthday present, online. Will you go halfsies?"

"Sure. A present for her, a drama degree for you. Excellent move."

"I don't hate her anymore."

"Come on, kid. It's me."

"Fine. Think what you want."

After a minute:

"You really don't hate her?"

"We've been having fun."

"Do you love her?"

"Maybe. I don't know. But it's easier not hating. Hating's hard."

*

"Kay. Made my wish."

We're in the kitchen. All of us. Henrik's asleep at the table, in his party hat. Lynette's leaning over her birthday cake. She blows the candles out."

"Whooooo."

She frowns at me.

"Didn't work. He's still here."

She begins slicing the cake. Scattered on the table are her opened presents. From Henrik, a bag of dates. Eddie got her some new jeans. Diana and I, a boxed *Grateful Dead* CD set, which I paid for. Lynette stops cutting. She takes a hard breath.

"I just wanna say that I'm pretty damn lucky. As much as I tried to screw my life up, it's still here. Eddie, Diana, I love you so much it hurts and all I can promise is, the rest of our time's gonna be a damn sight better'n the before."

Eddie starts laughing.

"Remember when we were racing that Turpin guy to the Canadian border."

"Yeah...well, that wasn't real funny."

But Lynette has to hide a snicker. She says to me:

"He was a State Trooper and our landlord and resident Peepin Tom, when we scrammed without payin the rent cause he never would fix the damn toilet."

"She had me steering and she was half out the window, trying to shoot out his tires."

Diana starts laughing. It sounds like music.

"Remember, Diana?"

"I was screaming over and over, *We're gonna die. We're gonna die.*"

"And mom said…"

He can't go on. He's cackling too hard.

"I said…"

Lynette can barely talk.

"I said…I'd be willin to go to hell, just to pee indoors."

All three of them double over in the pure joy of past pain. Lynette wipes her eyes, then raises her coke bottle.

"Here's to the good old, bad old days. May they never happen again."

We all drink.

*

"Yanga!"

"Yanga din."

"Animawa!"

I roll off her and we both lay dog-panting on the bed.

"All right. Maybe a two-time thing."

"Jesus, Lynette. You were…Vesuvial."

"Ditto you, stud. Ain't been that wild since Olaf the circus strongman spanked me with a loofah brush."

"What happened? One minute we're eating cake, the next minute, each other."

"I'm feelin good. When I feel good, I get horny."

She snags her cigs and lighter. I rip them out of her hand.

"Hey!"

"I hate these things. You smell of cancer. If you're determined to commit suicide, at least have the courtesy not to take me with you."

"I ain't gonna die."

"Yes, you are. You'll waste and wither until they slide your body under a mortuary door."

"Ain't you Mr. Sunshine."

"Do what you want, Lynette. Just don't kid yourself."

She gives me a new expression. It's…earnestness?

"Why do you care what happens to me?"

"I don't. I told you I'm concerned for my own health."

She holds her expression. It makes me uncomfortable.

"I never thanked you for helpin out with the Diana crisis. Or Eddie's school deal. So…thanks."

"I didn't do anything."

"Yeah, you did. For a nut box, you got a real handle on what makes those kids tick."

"I don't know about that."

"You ever miss not havin parents?"

I blink.

"How do you know about that?"

"Diana. We share everything, now."

"They kicked off when I was four. Can you miss what you never had?"

"My ma run off. Pop worked oil rigs, all over Texas 'n Oklahoma. Got laid off a lot, 'n slapped me around whenever he did. So, when I was fifteen, I ran away to find my own fella to beat on me."

She reaches for the cigarettes that aren't there. She drinks some water instead.

"I had to pass three written tests and two road ones to drive rigs. How come there ain't no quiz for bein a parent?"

"Excellent question."

We lay there, in silence, pondering mysteries whose answers are too complex and elusive for us to grasp. After a few minutes of this, I say:

"I'm having second thoughts about becoming a porn star."

"Come, again? Oops…"

She giggles.

"Tonight, I was watching all of you, and I thought, what if I have a family someday? Porn gets all over the internet. Do I want my children watching me wag Little Paul all over their monitor? Do I want the neighbor's kids calling my son names like…Dick Tater-Tot?"

"You want a family?"

"I didn't say that."

"You asked it."

"My point is, porn is such a seedy business. Semen flying everywhere and I'm so fastidious, I'd have to wear four or five rubbers and a mouth dam and…I'm beginning to think this idea wasn't very well thought out."

"Quinlan…"

"Don't wise crack. I'm warning you."

"I was just gonna say you might be, for a change, finally using your head for more than a hair-holder."

"Thank you. Maybe I'll be a fireman."

"I was wrong."

"Or a clown. Bring joy to children."

She sits up.

"Do you hear yourself? Do you know how outta control you are?"

"No! I don't! I'm too out of control to have any sense of how out of control I am."

"You don't take a deep breath, you're gonna find yourself in the damn French Foreign Legion, buster, and you can bet every one of them mothers smokes up a storm, and non-filters."

I sigh.

"You're right."

"I'm always right, with you."

"I can't help myself. Where I worked...who I worked for, for years...it was all manipulation. Figuring the angles. That's what I know how to do. But, finding my way to some sort of meaning or true purpose? It's...my mind just won't take me there, and frankly, you've shown very little sensitivity to my situation. You still think I'm rich and spoiled, right? That's it, isn't it?"

"No, I think you're rich and really screwed up."

"Well, I am, but, but... look. You were having a grand

old time with the parties and the drugs, right? But you really weren't. Something inside you was telling you to change your life. Become a better person. Isn't that true?"

"Pretty much."

"Lynette, that's all I'm trying to do. Become a better person."

She chews on this.

"You're sure pickin the hard way to do it."

"You know an easy way?"

"You can't figure everything out ahead of time, Quinlan. Whyn't you just live your life, stead of tryin to think out how you should live it?"

"What does that even mean, 'Just live your life?' I have to *do* something. I'm not a plant."

"You're all tied up in knots, dude. Chill out. Let it come to you. Might be closer'n you think."

"My god. That's so…"

I hesitate because I distinctively felt some microwave "ding" inside me, when she said what she said. Something deep inside me whispering, "This is worth considering."

"Well…it's interesting."

"I got my moments."

"You're telling me, if I understand you correctly, that I've been too focused on results, on trying to force things, but what I really need to do is slow down, so I can hear the beckoning and clarion call of the universal wisdom that will surely lead me to the peace and fulfillment I so desire, if I only let it."

She sighs.

"I just said do nothin. You, as usual, are off to Mars with it. Jesus, Quinlan."

"My god! This is it. The secret, revealed. I know what to do, which is, not do it. Thank you, thank you, Lynette, for your advice. That is absolutely brilliant in its simplicity."

"That's how I work. You wanna fool around some more?"

"No. I have so much to think about."

"There you go, again. Not this time, kiddo."

She rolls atop me and starts dry humping.

"What about this only being a two-time thing?"

"This is therapy. Love me up, baby. Love me for your own peace of mind."

*

Nothing. The Zen deal. My answer. Of course. You want to make God laugh, tell him your plans, right? You can't grab ahold of Fate. It's always a step ahead. Always. You must stand still, let Him/Her/It come to you. Embrace what is meant to be because it will anyway, won't it? Yes, stillness, silence. Of course, actually doing nothing is problematic because everything you do to do nothing is, by definition, something. Nevertheless, I hunkered in my stall all the next day, avowed to eliminate every shred of stimulus. I sat on my cot, cross-legged. I relaxed…relaxed. Then, I yelped and hopped around the room cursing, as a rope-twisting, thigh-vising charley horse garroted my left haunch. Eventually, with some very focused deep breathing and six pinpoint punches to the spasm's solar plexus, it gave up the ghost and I lay back on the bed, extremely straight-legged. I unwound. Let go. Just was. I found myself focusing on Moose. I slowly began softly repeating my mantra:

"Mooooose…Moooooose."

And, I drifted far, far away. I became fluffy, billowy. A pillow of air. Lighter than light. It was perfect. I was perfect. There was nothing I had to become. I was all.

I was love. I was peace. I was being attacked by a bee! I leapt up, again, flailing my arms like a '60s go-go dancer. He was dive-bombing me, a black and yellow kamikaze, murder in his beady bee eyes. I ducked, then batted him. He started zig-zagging, crazily, eventually loop-looping to the ground and spun in spastic circles, reminding me of myself. I jumped up and down on him 18 times, not stopping until all the internal organs of that crazed killer were safely outside his body.

I tried to empty, again, but blissing out is almost impossible with dead bee blood on your hands...or feet...so I went over to the house and scarfed down a liverwurst sandwich with a big pickle. While trying to pry some lunch gunk out of my teeth with a potato peeler, I realized this "nothing" business isn't going to work for me. I'm a people person. I learn from human interaction. Maybe if I just keenly observed others, I might gain the insight I yearn for. Sure. I'm so self-involved, but a wise man learns by listening. A wise man knows that everyone has something to teach him, if he just remains open to that possibility. I don't know why Lynette insisted I try this Zen stuff. Sometimes I think she's got a screw or two loose.

*

Lynette makes a quick run to Houston. Diana drops more and more of her attitude and it's decidedly less fun giving her grief. Eddie and I double our study hours. My golf game gets sharper and sharper. Miraculously, I do not decide I will now become a member of the PGA Tour. Certain that my road to self-knowledge runs through others, I'm keeping my spiritual ears wide open and wax-free.

I'm in the grove with Henrik, helping him pick more dates. Dates, I now realize, grow on trees. Date Palm trees. We are uncomfortably high in the air, or I am anyway, on ladders that lean on adjoining trees. He's a machine, plucking ten dates to my one. Silently. Inscrutably. The only words he's said to me in the hour we've been here were, "Watch out for da rats," just as I reached into the thorny palm crown and causing me to jerk backwards and slide halfway down the ladder, almost setting my thighs on fire. But...look at him. An automaton. He's the same. Always. What drives him? What does he want? Does he feel? He doesn't seem unhappy. He doesn't seem anything. But he is, everyone is…something. Perhaps in his quasi-consciousness he knows things, as in the way, for example, a worm knows how to crawl. Perchance he is The Wise Fool. Unlikely as it seems, he may hold the missing piece in my existential jigsaw puzzle. I've got to know more about this geriatric ubermensch.

"Henrik."

"Hunh?"

"What's the secret?"

"Hunh?"

"You've seen your share of things. What's it all about?"

"Don't talk. Vork."

I pick a date, slipping it into the burlap sack that's around my shoulder. He picks forty.

"Were you ever married?"

"Nein."

"Why not?"

"Dis ain't da quiz show. Pick. Pick."

I pick two dates. He picks a hundred.

"What was the happiest moment of your life?"

"Vass?"

"Are you happy, now?"

"Dot's enuff."

He begins to descend the ladder. I do, also.

"Do you find meaning in your work? Do you have a spiritual component?"

Twelve feet above ground, he hops off the ladder. I don't. I cautiously one-rung-at-a-time myself back to the earth as he's emptying his sack into one of several crates already loaded down with dates.

"Do you believe in life after death?"

"Grab da boxes."

I empty my sack, then pick up one of the large date hoppers. I can barely lift it. Henrik stacks one basket on top of another, hoists four of them as if they're Twinkies and moves off. I call after:

"What's for dinner?"

*

Luther's showing me around his workshop. His being Native American, I hoped he might, despite the fact that his hook is worse than ever, possess some enlightening spiritual secrets he could share. Luther is, apparently, some manner of artist. He's got these amazingly horrible wood "creations" sitting around. Piles of former trees that inspire nothing so much as an intense desire in me to take an ax to them.

"I was raised in the old ways. This existence is merely a test. Preparation for the afterlife. You like this one?"

He points to a revolting wood sculpture that seems to portray a squid playing Twister with an octopus. It's all I can do to stifle a gasp.

"*The Joyful Heart.* Commissioned for twenty-five thousand. I'm big in Europe, now."

"Mmm. So, where do you get your ideas, Luther?"

"From my dreams, of course. Where all truth resides. This one here?"

He indicates another sculpture. I would call it, *Cat Licking Exhaust Pipe.*

"*Summer Idyll.* Sorry, it's sold. Fifteen K."

"Mmm. So, this is what you dream about, huh?"

"Oh, yes. Listen to your dreams, Mr. Paul. Live them, live them. For they connect to all the wisdom of the ages. To Dante and Leo Buscaglia. Only by understanding that can man live in harmony with all of nature. Be nature. Be the wind…be the cricket. Then, when you die, you will flow like Karo syrup into the Land of Real Life, where all is sweetness and honey and love grows on trees. Made another one of this baby, here, last year…"

He indicates a worm-holed monstrosity. *Stalin Mates Goat?*

"*Song of Spring.* Bought me my Range Rover."

*

I talk to several more people, to no avail. Lucy Redspot, at the Big Mart, who says when she's down she makes maize chutney and suggests I try it. Our date distributor, an extremely wide man with the unlikely name of Sam Hill, reported he's always happy which he attributes to smoking a joint every day of his life for the last 37 years. Right. Drugs. That's the ticket.

In desperation, I began accosting strangers asking them what the meaning of life is. The ones who didn't run away or threaten me with a shotgun usually responded with something containing the word "God" in it. "God has a plan." "God wants us to be good." "God knows the answers." Even Eddie had once mentioned to me that part of the Twelve Step Program has to do with accepting the existence of a Greater Power. Now I would love to believe there exists some Big Guy or Gal, somewhere, who is going to ultimately make everything alright, but I am cursed with an inability to blindly accept anything. I have a mind and it is on my shoulders to be used. The great thing about having no questions is you need no answers, but I have questions. What's with the floods and earthquakes …dead babies…murderous dictators…Yanni? "Oh, there's a reason for it all." What reason? Where is it written down? The Bible? What if Matthew, Mark, Luke and John were all their respective village idiots, earlier versions of the guy outside my old office building who wore newspaper hats and claimed his shoes could fly? How can anyone be content in this hall of mirrors? It's surrealistic. No one else seems to really ponder on what they are doing or why. Why is everyone other than the odd philosopher just…living? Why don't they see it makes no sense? Jesus, what a Pandora's box I've opened up. Is there no answer, ever for me? Will I run around in figure eights for years with all my questions, then one sunny day, while taking a dump probably, feel this tug in my chest? And then, the tug becomes a vise and I open my mouth but nothing comes out and I become warm and cold at the same time and I glide in slow motion to the floor, and before I can even wipe my ass, everything starts to seem far away and foreign and my last thought before the shade is drawn, my very last synapse in this strange and curvy life is… "Wait a minute, I've got it." Glunk. Or perhaps there is no "aha" moment to be had. Ever. Maybe it really is just a series of random incidents, signifying nothing. How is one to know? Why is it all so secretive? Why is it one of those crossword puzzles with no black squares? Jesus, six or ten billion people on this planet and nobody knows why they're here. Pretending that it matters if their lawn has crabgrass. Running around on a great big ball of mud, grasping, truly grasping one and only one thing…one day they won't be. Ooh, sorry Lynette, am I thinking again? Well, what the hell sort of life is this, if the only way you can get through it is by *not* thinking or…or abrogating all personal responsibility to some sort of shadowy and silent "Maker." No wonder I was so obsessed with my career. It's something real, something you can measure yourself against. I work, therefore I am. But the rest of it is just a big underexposed blur…we're all passengers on an airplane going down. Decay. Slow rot. Rust never sleeping. I'm not making this up, that's the way it is. I'm not nuts, they are, but…well, everybody else is sure having a better time than me, so who's the real idiot? Sam Hill gets stoned and watches the sunset every night and enjoys himself. I don't enjoy anything. Not only do I have to die, but I'm not even capable of enjoying life while I'm alive. I'm…I'm…losing track of what I'm talking about. It's so…circular. It's just…I want some sense, dammit. I want to feel it matters what I do, which I don't now because…because… I …goddam! How did I get into this bunker? Why is it that every attempt I make to escape only leaves me further underground? Who is it…who, why…that is punishing me?

At present, I'm on hold. Everything's in abeyance. Listening to the clock tick. They say if you get lost in a forest you're supposed to stay where you are. It increases your chances of being found. So, here I am. I'm waiting. Hello? Anyone there?

✳

Lem's driving me home from the course in her Nissan.

"Quinlan, you played near dead-on perfect golf."

"I wasn't too shabby."

"Not shabby? You think Luther dubs just anybody, 'Dances with Ernie Els'?"

"Maybe it has something to do with not caring."

"Not caring about what?"

"About anything. I'm supposed to be on a voyage of self-discovery, but I can't get the ship out of the harbor."

"Oh well, those big questions can get you scratchin your head, all right."

"Especially when the guy scratching is a freaking moron."

"You ain't so bad, Quinlan. You ain't bad as most."

She's pretty cool. People are drawn to those who are at ease with themselves. I know all about being comfortable with yourself because I used to pretend to be that way at my job. Disarm the foe, then steal his fillings. But, Lem isn't feigning anything.

"I wouldn't mind being more like you."

Her water balloon boobs bounce as she chortles.

"You wanna be an aging bull dyke, who's 40 pounds overweight?"

"You're content."

She's a careful driver, checking her rear and side mirrors often. Or maybe that's just what cops do.

"I'm from Springfield Mo, originally. Buckle of the Bible Belt. Never felt comfortable expressin my true nature there. Headed down to Florida, after high school. Expressed myself plenty. Fast life. Parties twenty-four seven. Thought I was doin real kosher til one night I found myself on the roof of the Shangri-La Hotel and wantin to jump off. Next day, I booked back home. Sat my daddy down and said, 'Poppa, I'm a lesbian.' He cried and yelled and waved the Good Book and disowned me and all that stuff. Then, after about a week of the silent treatment, he shuffled up to me in the garden and he said he didn't understand me at all, but he loved me anyway. And we hugged. And ever since then, yeah…I think I am pretty content."

"Mmm."

"Well, whatta we got here?"

Up ahead, an old clunker with a flat tire is thumping along at about 30.

"That Chivvy matches one used takin down Slim Fat's Wraps, over in Wheels, yesterday."

"Wow."

"Slink down in that seat Quinlan, whilst I see what's what."

She pulls alongside the car. Driving it is a mountain with ears. Full beard, crazy hair.

"Howdy, there. Pull over. I'll help you with the tire."

The gun appears in a flash.

"Eat the seat, Quinlan!"

I duck down. Lem, just as fast, cranks her steering wheel, bangs the Chevy. The gun flies out of the car. Mountain man brakes. He's out the door and sprinting across the desert. Lem slams to a halt and is after him in two seconds. Mountain Man's 300 pounds of slow brisket. Lem's got him in 50 yards. I'm out of the car, trailing behind as she jumps his back and wrangles him to the ground. He's strong, pushes her off. He grabs a rock and goes after her. That's when I jump him.

"Dang, it, Quinlan. Get your civilian butt back in the car."

Not a chance. The three of us roll around in the sand. In an inspired moment of idiocy, I leap up, run back and forth across him three times and then give him The Rock's famous "People's Elbow." He wheezes, starts throwing wild punches in the air. Lem gets her cuffs out. I throw sand in his mouth. He gags, long enough that Lem can just get a cuff around his massive wrists. He tries to kick her. Adrenaline red-lining, and after preening a bit for the fans, I propel myself six inches into the air and cannonball fatso's belly with my butt. He blows out a fart equal in velocity to all of Aunt Ina's for 40 years. Seems to take the wind out of him, so to speak.

"Not fightin, no more."

He lays, arms splayed out, passive. I'm amazed. What did I do? Was that me? Lem stands. Pulls her gun. Her left leg almost gives way and she has to favor it.

"Coulda got your head blowed off, moron."

"I had to help, Lem."

"I meant him, Quinlan."

"Oh."

He could be dead. If it had been anyone but Lem.

"Bring the car around, Quinlan. Gonna have to take

a jail detour getting you home."

I run back to the Nissan, hearing, as I do:

Pffflllttt!

"You stink up my Nissan, tellin you now I'll put a hole in your foot!"

We get Rip Snorter locked up. The sheriff's office is...strange. It's large. Huge. Five times bigger than necessary. Vaguely Scandinavian architecture. Swinging double doors.

"Former House of Pies."

Says Lem.

*

Taking me out to Lynette's, Lem is not happy.

"Time was, I woulda taken that oaf down with one good right."

"Jesus, Lem. He's a giant."

"This is a young person's job. You start needin citizen assistance, you gotta reassess."

"I understand. But I gotta tell you, it was pretty exciting for me."

"You acquitted yourself admirably back there, Quinlan."

"I enjoyed having someone to take my frustrations out on."

"Specially like that belly bounce. Might have to give you some Sheriff's Helper Award, or somethin."

"I'd settle for you just going easier on yourself."

"You really had a romp, huh?"

"It's the most fun I ever had with clothes on."

She laughs out loud.

"Me, too."

*

It's late in the day and I've taken a walk out into the desert. I think I'm becoming acclimated to microwave level heat. The sun feels good, there's a hint of breeze. I take my shirt off and enjoy my surroundings. It's funny. If you stare at the desert long enough you begin to see colors. At first it all seemed khaki to me, but now, there's pink and blue. Purple. It's pretty in its own way. Maybe even beautiful. I feel safe under the soft canopy of sky. I'm protected here, in this place. Or maybe I just feel I don't have to be anything other than I am. Just letting it come to me, as Lynette said.

I consider Lem's words. How she had this big, closed door between her and what she could be, until she dealt with her father. Makes sense. If you can't go forward, maybe something behind is holding onto you. Or me. Could this be what my open-ear policy has been leading me to? Is this what I've needed to hear? My equivalent of Lem's father would be, of course…

"Agh!"

…Bud. Do I have unfinished business with him? Must I psychically slay my own personal dragon to truly free myself? Must I stare…

"Agh!"

…Bud right in the eye and tell him off? No. What would it accomplish, besides his figure-four-leg-locking my head and then twisting my gonads til they popped? Mmm. Okay…it might help. I did slink away with my nose between my legs. What kind of a message does that send to myself? That I'm a coward. That I have to hide in the shadows to be the real Paul. Well, dammit, the world belongs to me, too, and even though it's true that…

"Agh!"

…Bud doesn't deserve the respect of my attention.

This is a chance to make a personal statement. My own personal Emancipation Proclamation. Jesus. Yes. Yes. I have to do this.

"Agh!"

Not now. Calm down, Paul, it's okay. Not anytime, anywhere near soon. Man. He'd steamroll me. Have me convinced in thirty seconds that doing it to them before they do it to you is the real Golden Rule. I have to be stronger than I am now. Really, really buff. I'll work on it. Prepare for that guy like a DMV test. Always hated those things. I'll start organizing my thoughts...that, in itself, will be an accomplishment. I'll create a "Why Bud Sucks" paper. I'll study it, rehearse my performance. Then, when my car is ready and I am protectively suited in layer upon layer of logical and emotional armor, I will do it. I will do what I know I must. I will return to L.A. I will face and, I am confident, face down...

"Agh!"

...Bud.

"You're gonna tell this guy off."

"Right. What do you think?"

We're in the living room. Lynette and I. She's

watching a show that's titled, "Your Front Yard: Eden on a Budget." It's spelled out on the screen in flowers.

"I think I might dress this place up a bit."

"I mean about what I'm going to do."

"Oh. Thought you didn't want me buttin into your shit."

"Well…I've made some, shall we say, questionable choices of late."

"Shall we say 'stupid'?"

"I just feel it's wise to bounce my thoughts off someone. Work with a net, as it were."

"A-hunh. Well, my way is 'past is past' and best forgot. You put yourself in gear 'n go forward."

She illustrates this with a hand that goes, presumably, forward.

"You don't think what you've done before affects the present?"

"Yesterday's a dead dog."

"But everything you're doing now, your whole life, is an attempt to make up for your errors of the past."

"Thought we was talkin about you."

"I'm making a point."

"I blew it. Big time. I gotta make up for it. There ain't

shit wrong with you, or anythin you got to prove, except what you're making up in that monkey mind."

"I'm trying to find my place. And something's in the way."

"Not necessarily."

"What's that mean?"

"Nothin."

"Every time you say nothin, you mean something."

"Look. You wanna leave here and showdown your old boss. Do it, I don't care. After that you can find that kid who used to steal your lunch money, 'n after that some teacher who gave you a bad grade. But, sooner or later, you've got to stop 'then' and start 'now.' Take what's in front of you and do the best you can with it. Course, I ain't no expert, as you were so kind to remind me of, so what do I know?"

She returns her attention to the TV. No words occur to me. We sit there.

"If you're done talkin, I wanna have a cigarette."

I stand and walk out of the room. Why's she so testy?

*

"You nervous?"

"Yeah."

"Good. That means all your synapses are percolating. I never closed a big deal when I wasn't fighting an urge to heave."

"In that case, I should get a perfect score."

I laugh. He grins. It's test day. We're at the school. Lynette's on her way home, to return later in the day. It's up to me to pump this kid up with a gung-ho, Anthony Robbins Personal Power speech that will inspire him to a soaring feat of unequaled brilliance.

"So…good luck."

"Thanks."

He heads for the room. That was pathetic. I run after him.

"Eddie."

He stops. I put my hand on his shoulder.

"Really, really good luck."

"Thanks, Paul."

He goes into the room. I feel much better.

*

Eddie passes the test. He does so well, he's double-promoted to the seventh grade, the class he would've been in without the two-year binge. Lynette's ecstatic, jumps my bones to prove it. So athletically, that, as she orgasms I'm catapulted off the bed. While I climb back onto it, she says:

"I'm gonna throw a party to celebrate. We'll invite the whole gang."

"Jesus, I wrenched my back."

I gently ease myself down on the mattress.

"That Eddie's somethin. You shoulda seen him a coupla years ago, Quinlan. Wasted, he was."

"Do you have a heating pad?"

"He couldn't 'a done it without you, Quinlan. Hell, you're ship-shapin the whole damn family."

"Ah. I think I pinched a nerve."

"Roll over. I'll work it out for you."

"I can't roll over, I'm in agony...yatz!"

She rolls me over, begins kneading my spine.

"Oh, god. That hurts. Stop. No. Don't stop. Hurts good. Anh!"

"Quinlan...?"

"What?"

"Nothin."

"There you go, again."

"You wouldn't never hit me, would you?"

"Ooh. What?"

"Punch me. Slug me."

"Of course not."

"Good.

"Why would you even ask that?"

"Cause I don't take no shit, no more."

"Agh! Agh! I believe you!"

*

Henrik informs me we need track lighting in the kitchen. It's too dark in there, the proof being that last night he put cotton balls in his seafood bisque. I begin my Bud Notes at my computer. Well, begin might be a slight, semantical overstatement. "Not begin" would be more technically accurate. Just dwelling on…Him, I get addled and queasy. I burp. I sweat. I feel an overwhelming desire to stand at attention. I'm too chicken shit to even deal with Him in a word processor, 800 miles away. It's all I can do to write a word, any word. I finally manage to get one down: "Stomp."

*

"I wish I'd hear from SC."

"Mommy."

"What?"

"They turn you down, sic her on the Registrar. If he appreciates his jaw facing forward, you're in."

"I really want to get admitted on my merits."

"Diana, I was once a player. Always have a fallback strategy."

I look at her. She's grinning, goofily.

"I feel so...unprisoned. Freed from the poison of anger and rage, I now can accomplish anything."

"Huh."

I try to internalize her vibe, without prejudice. It's a good one. It's a sitar playing "Hava Nagila." I take the plunge.

"I'm somewhat trying to free myself."

"Groovy."

"I'm Microsoft Wording some things down, to say to someone. It's...slow going."

"I sense fear."

"I'm not afraid. Merely petrified."

"Why don't you talk to me as if I were the person you're so terrified of?"

"I don't want to."

"I think you do. You must face your demons or be nailed to their cross forever."

"Where are you getting this stuff?"

"Our new cheerleader leader is an Esalen grad. So…what is the name of this horrid person standing between you and self-realization?"

"Agh!…Bud."

"All right. I'm Aghbud. Tell me off."

"Um…well…okay."

"Good."

I say nothing.

"I'm waiting."

"Would you mind looking out the window?"

*

"Let me get you a cart, Lem."

"Don't need no cart, Quinlan."

She's gimping. Been gimping since going mano y lesbo with Mountain Man.

"Maybe you should go see Doc Gooden, over in Avalon, Lem."

"Rayno, shut up and go find your ball."

She hobbles up the fairway. We watch her struggle. Luther approaches.

"She ain't gonna make it to eighteen."

"Luther, you got some tribal hoodoo could ease her pain some?"

"I could try imbuing her with the spirit of the wolf."

"Do it quiet, or she might slug you."

"Yeah. Silent wolf."

Luther hustles off, in pursuit of Lem.

"She needs a real doctor, Rayno."

"Luther's got some powerful medicine. Singled my double vision after I dove into that empty quarry. Say, I talked to some guy, Jean Loooey in Montreal, bout your ka-jarta."

"But he didn't have it, right?"

"His exact word was 'non,' so I wouldn't be expectin no news flash, toot sweet. That's French. Hey, check it out, Luther's doin his thing."

Indeed. Ahead, as Lem lines up a shot, Luther stands behind her, gesturing and silently moving his lips.

"Hope Luther knows the difference between wolf and werewolf."

"Rayno?"

"Yeah?"

"Go find your ball."

*

Lynette prepares for "The Big Soiree." At night, I'm starting to ream Mr. Big Stuff, but good. My school-bound role playing with Dr. Diana continues and she's become an uncanny B Man stand-in. Yesterday, she called me a sniveling jellyfish, then ripped my watch off my wrist and kept it. But, later that night, I snuck into her purse and stole it back along with a pack of lemon drops, so I feel I'm getting stronger every day. Lynette tells me she wants to take Eddie to his first day of junior high. That morning I escort him out to the pickup.

"Piece of cake, Ed."

"It's been a long time since I was in my own grade."

"I remember when I had to make my first solo presentation. In my old job. First, I guzzled a whole bottle of Pepto Bismal. Then I went to the conference room, but my hands were sweating so much that I couldn't open the door. Finally, I did and there're these five guys in there. They've all got their arms folded and I know they know I'm a punk and I'll never make the sale. And my lip is trembling, and my hands are shaking and I am ready to chuck it all and just run out of that room. That's when I notice this one fellow. He reminds me of Frankie Rappaport. Frankie was the dumbest kid in my old neighborhood. He was so stupid he couldn't tie a pair of loafers. And I thought to myself, hey, maybe you can't make a pitch to these hard asses, but how about Frankie? So, I started my spiel, imagining it was that moron Frankie I was talking too and before I knew it, I was done."

"Did you make the sale?"

"Not a chance. But I knew, from that moment on, that no matter how bumpy things got, I could handle it."

He mulls.

"How come I can be so brave about some things and so cowardly about other things?"

198

"You figure that one out, let me know."

"Yeah."

He opens the truck door. Lynette's at the wheel.

"See you at three, kid."

"Thanks again, Paul."

I wave it off. He gets in the truck. Lynette pulls out. I call after:

"Find a Frankie."

*

Party day arrives. As the weather is unseasonably tepid, and with the rock providing sun cover, we set three card tables up on the front yard with gravel and drape bed sheets over them. Lynette's made up a paper towel banner reading, "Eddie...You Da Bomb," and strung it on the house. Henrik prepared something he called "Shrumknudel." I provide refreshments. Lem arrives, hobbling, with a female friend named Wicked Wanda, a postal employee who is six foot tall and weighs 40 pounds. Rayno shows up with his squeeze du jour, Janelle, another postal employee who is five foot tall and 300 pounds. Henrik brings the food out.

The day becomes even more gala, when Diana opens a letter Wanda brought her and finds out:

"Oh my god! I'm going to the University of Southern California!!"

Screams. Estrogen flying everywhere. Eddie slaps Diana on the back. She cries. Lynette cries, blurting:

"My baby's matriculated!"

Arnold Palmers for all. Toasts. More toasts. We eat, we drink. We're all filled with mirth and shrump-knudel. Well, not Henrik, who, of course, falls asleep in his food and is dispatched to his quarters for a nap. And then, after Diana says we ought to re-name Henrik "Food Face," and we convulse for ten minutes, the merriment hits an even higher pitch. We play the home version of "Wheel of Fortune" and Lem wins an all-expense paid trip to Jamaica, declaring that she "loves dot, mon." And if that weren't enough, Janelle hauls out a Karaoke machine and Lynette belts out "Addicted to Love" and then somehow segues it into "Sunrise, Sunset" to which Rayno and Wicked Wanda get up and do-si-do, and Lem takes Polaroids of, for "prosperity." Then, we finale with cake and Neapolitan ice cream and, all in all, I have to say it is the most fun party I've ever attended which was held on gravel. A loving and well-deserved recognition of the indomitability and resurrection of Lynette's kids, and, I suppose, by extension, Lynette herself. She sure does look pleased, anyway. More than pleased. Relieved.

We wave at the two cars as the guests depart. They're not even out of sight when a Ford Explorer plods up the driveway road. Something menacing immediately pervades the air. The SUV stops about a hundred feet from us. A man emerges. A black man. Forty. Slim. He's dressed cowboy style.

"Jesus Joe Jones."

That's Lynette, who's ashen.

"Stay right here, children. Don't let him come near, Quinlan."

"Who is he?"

But she's already running for the house. Cowboy approaches. I meet him halfway:

"Hi, there."

"I don't want no trouble."

"Me, neither. What's your business?"

"Lynette knows my business."

He tries to push past me. I grab him. He pulls his arm

away. Then we both hear…

"One more step, they'll be callin you "No Knees Carl."

He stops. Lynette's coming off the stoop with a shotgun trained on him.

"Mom, what's going on?"

"Stay put, Diana. You, too, Eddie."

"I'm a different man, Lynette. Just five minutes, then I'll go. Please."

She steps up to him.

"Call 911, Quinlan."

She sticks the gun in his belly.

"Tell em somebody was breakin in and I had to shoot him seventeen times."

Carl backs up, but says loudly as he does:

"How are you, baby?"

To whom is he talking?

"Wanted to let you know I love you."

"Shut your damn mouth, Carl!"

He's at his car. Fear in his eyes. Nevertheless, he shouts:

"Daddy loves you, Diana."

And Lynette tries to take his head off with the gun

barrel. He half-deflects it with an arm."

"What's he saying, mom?"

"Nothin, Diana. He's just some drunk."

Lynette swings the gun again. Carl dodges it. He opens his car door.

"I woulda been around, daughter, but your mommy ran out and I couldn't find you."

Lynette swings again, gets him good this time, in the ribs.

"Oof. Check your birth certificate, child. Cooper, that's my name and yours, too."

Diana wrinkles her face. Then:

"Oh, god!"

"It's a scam, Diana. He wants money."

"Call me, honey. Call me. 818-760-3595."

He jumps into the car, avoiding another bash from Lynette, as Diana bolts.

"He's lyin, Diana. Don't listen."

But Diana runs into the house. Lynette hands me the gun.

"If he's here in ten seconds, blow his balls off."

She heads after Diana. I half-point the rifle at Carl, who's starting his engine.

"I'm goin. I'm goin."

He puts it in gear.

"But I know where she is, and I ain't lettin go of this. Tell Lynette that."

He slams it into reverse and drives backward, all the way up the road.

Diana locked herself in Lynette's bedroom. She dug out her birth certificate from Lynette's box under the bed and found out what Carl had claimed was true. She screamed through the door at Lynette, and by the time her mother had jimmied the door open, Diana had climbed out the window and was gone. The two of us fanned out, me in the pickup, Lynette in *Fightin Lady*. We searched for hours. Nothing. That evening, we got Lem on the job. The three of us were out all night, to no avail. About noon the next day, I came back to the house to see if there was any news. As I emerged from the pickup, a thought hit me.

She was asleep on the rock. I went down to the kitchen and dialed Lynette's cell phone. Then, Lem's. Then I climbed back up, in case Diana awoke and decided to take off. She was stirring as I arrived. She blinked. She saw me.

"I came up here to jump off."

"Why didn't you?"

"I still might."

"Your bed would be more comfortable than his."

"She told me my father died. My white father."

I say nothing.

"Why do people have children and do these things to them?"

"You're still the same person you were."

"I don't know who I am."

"You're going to SC. You'll be an actress."

"I want to kill her. I want to stab her in the eye."

"She might do it for you."

"Go away."

"No."

"I want to be alone."

"Sorry."

She stared out at the desert, for answers. None came. She laid her face on the rock and closed her eyes. I leaned towards her and whispered:

"You're very strong, Diana. You will find a way to hold this."

*

"Lemme go."

"You don't want to talk to her right now."

We're in the kitchen, struggling.

"Why? Because I'm a shit mother? Because I did everything you could do wrong, and was too stoned to know I was doin it? Because I don't deserve the gift of those two beautiful babies God blessed me with?"

She's vibrating.

"Because she's upset. Let her calm down."

"Course she's upset. Her mother's a sleep around whore. Why wouldn't she be upset?"

She paces.

"What if she jumps off the damn rock?"

"Henrik's up there."

"I can't take this."

She grabs her coat, heads for the living room.

"No!"

I follow her. She kitchen door-bangs me in the face, but I catch her in the living room and block the front door.

"Make a hole, Quinlan."

"You're not running away. No more."

"Why not? I can't do no good."

"You have to continue to be here. She'll see that. That's what parents are supposed to do. Be there. That's the requirement."

She hesitates. Her face ages about 10 years.

"Oh god, Quinlan."

She sags onto the couch.

"You pay for everything."

I place my hands on her shoulders.

"She's a survivor. She is. Eddie is, and they got that from you. They got your toughness."

I'm pleased with that statement. I let it sit in the air. Five seconds later:

"Really?"

"You will work this out. It will be better with everything in the open."

She considers this, then almost nods.

"Be patient. She'll come down."

She sighs.

"Gonna kill me, waitin."

She sighs, again.

"He had a hot butt and cool weed. Those was my only man requirements, back then."

"You're going to have to let him see her."

"Not if he's dead."

"He's hers, too."

"Or comatose."

"He is her father."

Silence. Then:

"You're right."

"I'm always right, with you."

Diana walks in.

"Oh, Jesus!"

That was both of us. She crosses to the bed, sits on it. She seems…peppy.

"So. I'm mulatto? Halle Berry, Mariah Carey mulatto?"

*

Henrik and I installed the track lighting. Okay, he put it up, I held the ladder. He didn't want my assistance because after Fred Quinne told him what Luke Bass told him that Big Terry's wife, Terri Terry, told him that Henry Hank told her what I did to Lem's septic line, he feared for our lives if I got near electricity. Eddie started playing pick-up basketball after school and made a couple of friends. One of them was named Frankie. I continued prepping for the Gunfight at the L.A. Corral, one night spooking a curious coyote as I gave my nemesis the tongue lashing of his life from the safety of a barn 800 miles from where he actually was. Oh, and Diana decided that being half-black was exotic and would afford her a certain cachet in her future performing career. She met with Carl who was, it seems, a famous rodeo bull rider. A famously bad bull rider. In truth, he was billed as "The World's Worst Bull Rider." In fact, "bull rider" is a misnomer because in 18 years he had never, not once, not been thrown from the bull, usually in the first two seconds. Bloodthirsty crowds would pack arenas to see him get gored and head-stomped and always come back for more, so he had an excellent income and that day with Diana, between blackouts, he offered to pay her complete college tuition.

In fact, Diana now found all of Lynette's younger indiscretions to be romantically bohemian and she followed her mother around the house all day, constantly asking, "And who did you screw then, Mom?" Go figure.

Lynette and I are strolling through the front yard/gravel quarry. She's very animated, talking mileaminute.

"Gotta domestic up this area. Show some pride of rentership."

"You might start with…"

"I'm gonna grab up a bunch a these rocks, paint em green and arrange em so they spell the word *Howdee*."

"Mmm."

"How*dee*. D-e-e. Cute, huh? Then I wanna throw a windmill in the middle and cactize all around it."

"Mmm."

"And hell, that should do it, right?"

I desperately want to say:

Lynette, you're a remarkable woman in many ways. You're utterly indomitable and hump like a man…in the complimentary sense of that term…but you have no taste. Your aesthetic sensibility is that of a barnyard animal. It's clunky, trashy, gaudy. It's more than gaudy. It's cliched gaudy and I hate it, hate it, hate it.

I say:

"That sounds virtually perfect."

"*Virtually*? What the hell kinda wiseass shot is that?

You think you know everything? I studied on this. Watched the H&G channel every damn day for three damn days, buddy-o."

I stare at her. She seems to catch herself.

"Sorry. I quit smokin and it's drivin me up the wall without a paddle."

"You quit smoking?"

"It wears on you. Never lets up."

"When did you quit?"

"Twenty minutes, it'll be an hour."

"Lynette, that's…wonderful."

"Yeah, I feel pretty good about myself. Ooh."

She grabs her belly.

"Crampin up a lot."

"Why did you decide to quit?"

"The way things are lookin up, family-wise, I figured I should take some health care."

"Watching your kids grow up is much easier if you're alive."

She grins, girlishly. She kicks some dirt around with her boot.

"Also, I guess you wouldn't mind not kissin a second-hand chimney stack, no more."

"I have felt somewhat smoked and cured at times, but...I'm so proud of you for making this commitment."

She's pleased that I'm pleased.

"It's the least I could do, after all you done for me 'n mine."

"It has been an interesting time."

"Sure has."

Lots of mutual smiling. Lynette again catches herself and hitches up her pants with her thumbs.

"So, about that windmill. Classic Dutch or high-tech?"

*

I'm hiking up the fairway with Rayno.

"So, I sent me a fax...which I had to drive to Horse Thief to do, but for which I ain't chargin you, cause I wanted some elk jerky, anyways...to Juan Don Dominguez, the head of all Mexican Swedish part distribution and he back-faxed me to say, and I quote, 'Ka-yarta, no,' so, all in all, we ain't lookin muy bueno. That's Spanish."

"Mmm."

I'm not paying attention. I'm observing Lem as she drives up to her ball in a golf cart. She hobbles out and limps to the back of it, where she grabs a club.

"How the mighty have fallen, eh, Mr. Paul?"

"How, indeed, Rayno."

*

"You took an impressionable, naive kid and filled his virgin heart with values scavenged from a toxic waste dump."

"Whoo! Louis L'Amour look out, there's a new kid in town."

Lem and I are in the Walter Hagen Grille, having an after-golf ginger beer and some of Rayno's gift pack of elk jerky. I'm reading excerpts from my first draft Bud harangue. If I concentrate ahead of time, I can say his name without flipping out now. Little victories.

Lem two-legs her chair, pushes her hat back on her head.

"You got a real flair for the poison pen word, Quinlan."

"I need it. Because only after I have attained Bud Closure, will I be able to, finally, put the past behind me and allow my true life's purpose to reveal itself."

"Interesting. I'm gonna tender my resignation."

"From here? The club?"

"From sheriff."

"What?"

"It's time."

"Are you sure?"

"This leg ain't gettin no better. Doc Gooden says it's arthritis. And my daddy's not doin that well. Figure I'll grab my pension and head back to Missoura."

"Who's going to be sheriff?"

"How bout you?"

I burst out laughing.

"Where did that come from?"

"After you clean up your beeswax in L.A., you come back. I'll show you the ropes for a couple weeks, then badge you up, and you, sir, will be the law for the entire unincorporated area west of Barranca Verde and east of Old Mule Trail."

"You're kidding, right?"

"I don't joke about who I turn my turf over to."

"I am totally unqualified to be a law enforcement officer."

"Not true. You whupped old Mountain Man to a molehill. And you're good with people, too, which is really what the job's all about."

"I'm not good with people."

"Don't be coy, Quinlan. Everybody knows you got Eddie promoted and Diana de-snobbed."

"I hate this horrid, barren desert."

"It's growin on you. Go away for a few days, you'll see. Every place else seems hectic."

"No, Lem."

"I took Wanda over to Laughlin for her eighth comin-out anniversary. Ooh, mama. Urban Jungle."

"I said, no."

"Did I mention you figure in benefits, you'll be takin down close to twenty grand per annum?"

"Lem, I don't want the job. You offered, I refused. Let it go."

"So, to summarize, you'll be well-paid, admired, borderin on idolatry, work in a roomy, well-lit place that smells of cobbler, with lots of counter space and an industrial freezer, and, to clinch the deal…"

She points to her head.

"You get to wear this spiffy hat."

It is spiffy. But, I lean in close to her.

"I've turned it down several times. You won't listen."

"You're the one, Quinlan. It's destiny. I can feel it in my calcified hip."

"Jesus. Get off it, Lem."

She leans into me.

"Know how I got this gig? I was just passin through and my car broke down."

She winks at me. I stand.

"I'll take my chances with destiny."

"I'll be keepin the offer open, Quinlan. Til right after you take the job."

"Good-bye, Lem."

"You wanna try on the hat?"

I walk away.

*

I drive back home, chuckling at Lem's bizarre suggestion. Becoming sheriff. Its absurdity boggles the mind. When I take a short nap before supper, it's completely erased from my thoughts. My conscious thoughts. I have a dream. I'm wearing the stetson, that startling accessory of justice, its silver star a beacon in truth's dark and stormy night but am otherwise buck naked. I'm slapping around some lowlife and screaming, "Where is she, punk? What's your brother done with J Lo?"

Awakening, I'm not too concerned. Being a cop is a common cowardly, mini-penised, white-male fantasy. Completely harmless. But the subject won't seem to go away.

*

"Okay. My three favorite all-time cop shows would be T.J. Hooker, Police Woman and the original Mod Squad."

Over chicken paprika and dumplings, Lynette's begun a conversation that's subject matter, I'm certain, was once stormily debated at the Algonquin Round Table.

"Now, Henrik, here, he's always made a strong case for Mannix."

She indicates Henrik, who is staring at me, his eyes wide open and snoring.

"Great hair, but strictly speaking, he was a P.I."

"What about Miami Vice?"

"A mite pastel for my taste, Eddie."

"I love NYPD Blue."

"Diana, any show that fills my 55-inch screen with Sipowicz's naked butt, I'm remotin. How bout you, Quinlan? You strike me as a Law & Order man."

"Why do we have to talk about police shows?"

"I'm trying to inject a little culture into our dinner chat, that's why. And cop dramas...well, they take in the whole range of human experience. They honor the fearless men and women whose only goal is to serve and protect."

"I love cops."

"We all do, Diana."

"I want to be a cop."

"That would swell the heart of any mother to tears, Eddie. So, Quinlan. What's your favorite cop show, past or present?"

"Homicide: Life on the Street."

"No. Too artsy."

"It was high quality."

"Oh, poop. It wasn't even as good a show with a

colon in it as Walker: Texas Ranger."

"Get outta here. Chuck Norris? With that Chia Pet beard?"

"Hey, he's the strong but…"

She snorts.

"…Chia Pet."

She laughs some more. It's infectious and the kids crack up, too. Henrik even seems to be grinning in his sleep. I'm not sure what's so funny, but I get caught up in the mirth, also. Lynette places her hand on mine.

"Quinlan, Quinlan. When you ain't loco, you are one hoot to have around."

*

In the morning, while chugging the kids to school, I find myself daydreaming that I'm in my sheriff's uniform and that big red light's on Saaby's roof. And everyone we pass gives an appreciative nod to me. Even Henry Hank offers a respectful salute with his pipe wrench. Then, after dropping my charges off, I vision-quest that I arrive home, after a hard day of foiling bank robberies and rescuing seven-toed kittens and the family gathers round me, wide-eyed, and forces the ever-modest Sheriff Quinlan to recount that day's heroic courage in melodramatic detail. Their faces glow, worshipfully, and Lynette, whose breasts have become even larger, says she's the luckiest woman in the world and then we eat buffalo burgers and tell jokes. We discuss Eddie's upcoming Being Sober Anniversary and Diana talks more about psychology, which she's developing quite the interest in, and I encourage her to…

"Agh!"

I crank the wheel to avoid a Joshua tree. It's spiny needles crawl in the window and roto-til my shoulder…

"Yahatz!"

As I barely avoid becoming a live crash-test dummy, I've daydream-driven into the desert. Jesus. I stop the truck. A prairie dog, raised half-out of his holey home, checks out the ruckus, then ducks back down to tell the wife and kids it's just another human out of control and how did they ever come to rule the world, anyway? I sit in the pickup and bleed and consider. What's going on? I'm consumed. By something it feels wrong to be consumed by. The thoughts I'm having are not my thoughts. I'm being mind-controlled somehow, and I don't care for it one bit. And now, at this very moment, my god…even while I'm insisting I don't want to be thinking about what I'm thinking about…I'm thinking about it, again. I'm seeing myself tracking some escaped con through this barren wasteland. He jumps out from behind a discarded Corvair and goes for me, just as a rattler rises up and does the same. But I dive to the side, the rattler's fangs sink into the desperado.

"Aah!."

This has got to stop, this…power of suggestion, that's what it is. That's what's going on. Yes. The *lesbian* power of suggestion.

∗

I push through the double swinging doors of the former House of Pies like a gunslinger. Lem is sliding papers into one of two large ovens which are now, apparently, used as filing cabinets. I stand feet wide apart, fingers twitching, ready to draw.

"I don't want to be sheriff."

As if expecting me, she continues filing.

"You mean, not yet."

"I turned down the offer."

"You can't turn it down, I'm keepin it open."

"Close it."

All she closes is the oven. Then limps over to her desk.

"What's wrong, Quinlan? You feelin pushed and pulled by somethin?"

"Only you. And if you think I'm going to spend the rest of my life wrestling drunks and fixing what Lynette and her crazy kids break…"

"Whoa!"

She turns to me.

"I think you added that last part on your own."

"It goes hand in hand, doesn't it?"

She grins.

"Only if you want it to."

"Which I don't."

"You 'n Lynette do make a cute couple, in a snake 'n mongoose kinda way."

"We're not a couple."

"I may shave my upper lip twice a week, but I'm still

a woman, Quinlan, and I sensed a spark 'tween you two right from the start."

"No. No sparking. You listen to me, Lem. I might be at a crossroads. I might be addled and make some comically wrong turns in trying to find myself, but I will. And when I do, it won't be languishing in a desolate, sand-baked town that doesn't even have a name, playing country cop and teaching children what their wandering mother never got around to. The solution to my problem is not taking on someone else's. So…back…off."

Lem leans on the edge of her desk. She folds her arms and peers into my soul, silently saying that I'll never, in 100 years, understand myself as well as she does.

"Stop that."

"Quinlan, I've grown right fond of you. I'd bet what you're tryin to find's right here in our no-frills dust barrel. But, you gotta turn that switch on yourself. So, I won't press you anymore. That's a promise. Whatever choices you make now, they're yours."

Why does that fill me with dread? Nevertheless, I've gotten what I came for. I say:

"Thank you."

I turn, take one step.

"Quinlan."

I don't turn back, but I do stop.

"Life is helpin."

I push my way out the doors.

That night, more mid-sleep drama. *Diva!!* in which I rescue J Lo from the hip-hop kidnapper who wants to marry her amazing butt. I crash, naked still, through the skylight of a Dunkin Donuts where she's being tortured by being forced to listen to her own music. The punk, temporarily blinded by the glint from my sheriff's hat star, lunges at me but his baggy pants are so low on his hips they fall down. He trips on them and I bash him unconscious with my erect penis and Jenny From The Block is so thrilled she offers me a giant churro and, just as I'm about to eat it, she rips off her face to reveal she's really Lynette and we start singing "Do Ya Think I'm Sexy?" Next, Diana and Eddie appear, doing Fly Girl moves and I wake and bolt out of bed, frantic, and then I sigh because it felt so good saving J Lyn. And then I scream because, in leaping up, I'd banged my knee on the cot post and then I smile because, even though I understand that real police work is seldom so dramatic and almost never conducted while starkers, it's so satisfying to feel good about myself, even if what I'm satisfied about is something I don't want. Or do. I don't know. I don't understand anything. God, my knee is throbbing. What's happening to me? I feel so vulnerable. Pressured. What is it? What's going on? I don't know. Yes. Yes, I do! Nature abhors a vacuum. That's what I've been. A Hoover vacuum. An empty vessel that anything could fill, even sleepy intimations of domesticity so unrealistic they're beyond discussion. I'm aimless, so any port in the storm seems desirable, even if the port's in a giant sandbox. The only antidote to this venomous lack of substance is to find myself. Right now. Tonight. If I can somehow hobble to an emotional Safe House...comprehend clearly, appropriately, what I'm doing, where I'm going, then nothing anyone here says or does can affect me. They, all of them, will be fried stuff to my Teflon. I have to do this. I have to. I must grab my laptop and check bookmarked sites from when I was originally planning to beat it out of here, some 14,000 years ago. Make some decisions. So…why aren't I moving? Why am I not stringing the phone line out to the house? Why am I recalling how much fun it was shooting hoops with Eddie two days ago? Why am I flip-flopping like an old pair of shower clogs? Why? Why?

"Hello, Paulie."

"Agh!"

I Air Jordan, pirouetting 180 degrees in mid-flight. I come down, face to face with my parents, sitting together on the cot. I quickly and cool-headedly realize I'm merely having another imaginary psychotic episode, which prevents me from totally freaking out. I experience a quick fit of shakes…

"Nyanya!"

And then, except for a recurring facial tic, I'm fine. It's nice to see them, to tell you the truth. They look the same as in photos I've seen. And…hunh…they're younger than me, now. Dad's in those dopey bell bottoms, with white shoes and belt. Muttonchop sideburns. Mom has long, straight hair, parted in the middle. Big glasses. A t-shirt that says, "I Think You *Ms.* The Point." Dad gives me a little salute.

"How's it goin, kiddo?"

"See, Roy? He's losing his chin, just like your uncle Hal."

Okay. What do you say to two dead parents who have just appeared in front of you?

"You guys...look terrific."

Dad chuckles.

"Well, we're not getting any older, sonny."

"Paulie, we've come to help with this big jumble of feelings you're experiencing."

"You have?"

"That's what parents do, right, Roy?"

"Yup. Though most of them are alive when they do it."

"Which is really the point, son."

"Yeah. Losing us at such an early age was the defining moment of your life, kiddo."

"But I don't even remember it. Or you."

"Your soul remembers. And that inner pain has prevented you, always, from forming any strong personal bonds. From giving your heart."

"You tried to fill that hole with lotsa money. Didn't work."

"Your need for authentic connection drove you away from L.A."

"And now you got a nice gang, down there. And that Lynette…"

Dad holds his hands out, suggesting Lynette's healthy chest.

"Hugga-mugga."

"But you're conflicted. Give of yourself and risk loss."

"Scary proposition for you, kid."

"Or stay safe but all alone."

"Bet you can guess which side we're on."

"Screw fear, Paulie."

"Well put, Lil. And you oughtta sing *The Paulie Song* once in a while, just as a mood lightener."

"What's *The Paulie Song*?"

"Oh, come on, you can't forget that. We'd sing it every night. Well, I sang. You ate fudge."

"I…don't…"

"It's okay, it'll come to you when you need it."

They sit there, satisfied, having apparently made their point. I'm somewhat less sanguine.

"Are you really here, or is this some mind game I'm playing with myself?"

"It's a mind game, silly. Dead people don't talk."

"But that doesn't change the truth of what we're not really here saying."

"My only memory of you is hearing you say you'd always be here to take care of me. Why should I listen to you now?"

"Oh, Roy. I told you he was angry."

"Hell, it ain't like we croaked just to spite him, Lil."

"You're his former father. Go on, say something wise."

"Yeah, yeah. Okay, look kid. When that boat sunk…when I was gurglin my last gurgle…in that final moment…the only thing that made the livin worth the water fillin my lungs and my kidneys blowin a gasket, was that I'd had mom and you to care about. When you gurgle, I want you to feel the same way."

"You don't have to be so graphic, Roy."

"I'm makin a point. You're a natural family guy, kid. Chance at redemption and all that. Don't blow it. You ain't no handyman. Okay, I said my piece, let's go, Lil."

He stands.

"All right, dear."

She stands.

"Go? No. You can't leave, already."

They hold hands.

"Good-bye, Paulie."

"Kid. Next time, our place. Hahaha."

"No. Mom. Dad. I've got a million questions to ask you."

But they start to fade away.

"Will I see you, again?"

"No, son. We only get one earthly visitation per eternity."

"We were halfway to Branson when your mom said you needed us. Had seats for Mel Tillis. Is that love, or what?"

They're almost gone.

"Learn to trust, Paulie. Bit by bit by bit."

"We got periodontitis in the genes. Floss, every day."

And, poof, there's nothing where they once were. The same as the other time.

*

I'm at the "Bye-Bye Bernie" website. On the message board. Reading the e-notes in the bottles of those cast adrift on the sea of life, of their own volition. From

Tangiers, they reach out. From Dar es Salaam. From Quito. But wherever these people write from, they don't write about where they are. They write about where they're going next. Where everything will be wonderful and all their dreams fulfilled. Desperation just under the surface. Cries from a crashed auto in a ditch at the side of the road. Souls apart, who try to fill their emptiness by becoming more alone. I think you don't have to be poor to be homeless. You don't have to be unemployed. Because home is not a place. Home is where, when you're not there, you feel like you should be. Or I guess it is. I've never felt I should be anywhere I've been. Do I, here? Is this what I've been seeking all this time? All my life? Is it that simple? Is that why Lynette smashed into me? I suppose I should try to find out. If it doesn't work out, I can always hit the road. Really no downside. Nothing to lose. No reason to be afraid. None at all. But, of course, I am.

*

"And, so I go, 'What about the safe driver discount?' And he goes, 'You ain't a safe driver.' And I go, '15 years 'n 1,000,000 miles.' I never killed no one yet."

Early morning. We're in the kitchen. I'm in Lynette's chair and she's "lowerin my ears." The chair's wobbling adds a touch of suspense to the proceedings.

"And he goes, 'You got three tickets the last three years.' And I go, 'No. One a them was dropped. Illegal speed trap. You better check your records.' So, he wiggled his computer and saw I was right, in black and white, and wrote me a two-hundred thirty-dollar rebate check on the spot, so's I figured I'd run us all over to Rutger, Saturday night. Couple hour jaunt but Buck's Ribs is worth it. Tastiest bones I ever sucked on. Well…almost."

She gives my shoulder a rub to emphasize the point. I open my mouth. No, I try to open my mouth. It's not easy. My lips want to stay shut. They've been shut too long, dammit. I blast them open with the pure energy of hope.

"Lynette, how would you feel about me sticking around after my car's ready? Ow!"

She's ice-picked my ear with her scissors.

"Sorry."

"Jesus Christ! You stabbed me!"

232

I grab my ear. She grabs a towel.

"Whadda you expect? You U-turn, you gotta signal first."

"Is it serious? Do I need stitches? Reconstructive surgery?"

"It's a scrape. Calm down."

I try to, as she dabs my ear with the towel.

"So, how come you wanna hang around, now?"

"I, uh…haven't decided where to go. Is it all right?"

"Sure. Kids'll be crazy excited to have you."

"And you?"

She seems to, suddenly, need to concentrate intently on her ear dabbing. She blots six, seven, eight times before responding, as casually and off-handedly as if I'd asked to borrow sugar.

"Guess I could handle it."

"Good."

"Hold that towel to your ear."

"Why? What're you doing?"

She's raising those glinting silver blades to my head, is what she's doing.

"Finishin up. You're uneven."

"Be very, extremely careful."

"Jeez, what a baby."

She resumes her trimming. It's nice. Very nice. Haircuts are comforting, somehow. I enjoy it for a moment and try to ignore that, in the mirror above the counter, my head now appears to be triangular.

"I never had a man be a friend to me, Quinlan."

"I guess that's what we are, huh? Friends?"

"I guess it is."

"Lem wants me to be sheriff. That's a laugh, huh? Ngah!"

She's lanced my other ear.

"Who are you, Sweeney Todd?"

"Quit droppin bombshells, mid-snip."

I grab a second towel. Put it to my other ear.

"I just mentioned it to you because it's so ridiculous."

"No, it's not."

"What?"

I can't hear her. Both ears covered. I remove the towel from my first punctured ear.

"What?"

"You'd be a crackerjack sheriff."

"I can't believe you're saying that. Why would I be a better sheriff than I would a handyman or a porn star?"

"You're good with people. That's what the job's really about. Long as you're not dealin with yourself, you're real smart and helpful."

"Oh."

"Sonofagun. Now, we got something real special to celebrate over at Buck's, Saturday Night."

"I'm not taking the job, Lynette. No way. What are you doing!?"

She's, again, pointing her Lynette Scissorhands at my head.

"Thought you might want more off the sides."

I peer into the mirror above the sink. Actually, I'm an octagon.

"I don't think it matters."

She squares my head up and studies it in the mirror.

"Mmm. Better leave it long. You got them Ross Perot ears."

I study my ears. They are big. Dumbo ears. Lynette pats my shoulder.

"But, they're cute."

That night we make love. For the first time. Really. All our bucking and thrashing is replaced by something quieter, softer and with much more meaning. I try to hide my face because, for some reason, I find myself crying. Lynette turns my face to hers.

"No more secrets."

She's crying, too. It feels good to cry with someone. It feels good to let go of something I've been dragging behind me for a long time.

"I'll be good for you," she whispers.

"I know."

The next morning:

"She's ka-jarta'd."

"Say that again, Rayno."

"Got one Sabe ready to go, Mr. Paul."

"She's ready? Saaby's ready?"

"Runnin like water downhill. Surprise!"

I drop the phone. Wow. I pick the phone back up.

"She's really ready?"

*

It's been a long time since I've felt so…unburdened. No. Wrong. I've never been this happy. No. I've never been happy. Ever. Not happy like this, when you're just feeling, I don't know…happy. I'm driving on air, as I transport Eddie, then Diana. They are delightfully self-centered at my announcement of my continued presence in their lives. Eddie asks if I can help him with his jump shot. Diana, having not only decided she will become a psychiatrist but a radio-call-in-psychiatrist, suggests that every day, henceforth, I should test her with a typical call-in query.

"Just pretend, you know, that you're more or less normal."

I stop by the gas station. Rayno will be dropping Saaby off later, but I'm so excited, I can't wait to see her. Her rising from the ashes seems to be a metaphor for my soul, which now, I'm almost too superstitious to say, I seem to have found.

"Yessir. She's spit, polished and spit, again."

Rayno and I are touring Saaby, who smiles happily in the sun. Her engine purrs. Her trunk is smooth and...

"Rayno, you even re-painted her. Beautifully. I can't even tell she was in an accident."

"Got me a top-secret ingredient I add to the filler. Hint: Denture Bond. Anyways, here's the totalled up bad news."

He hands me some paperwork.

"We don't bill 'surance, so you got to pay up and collect from them on the backside."

"Sure."

I flip through the various invoices.

"Sure gonna miss your gentlemanly golf company, Mr. Paul. Miss it more if I don't get that buck-fifty you owe me from our game Wednesday."

"I'm going to be sticking around, Rayno."

"Really? You mean permanent?'

"Could be."

Now Rayno cries.

"Rayno, why is this FedEx statement dated over a month ago?"

"Hmm?"

"According to this, the ka-jarta was delivered weeks ago."

"Nah."

I show him the paperwork.

"Yes. And your labor is billed just a few days later."

"I musta got mixed up, on accounta it's Leap Year."

He starts to whistle, casually. Too casually. I give him my Stern Teacher look. He shrinks like a microwaved orange.

"How long has this car been repaired, Rayno?"

"Is that the phone?"

He takes a step. I jump in front of him. He tries to go around me. I hand check him as if I were an NBA player on a seven-day contract.

"Why have you been holding out on me?"

"Oh, man…oh, man."

"Who put you up to this?"

"No, sir. No. I ain't no stoolie, again."

"If you don't tell me, I'm calling Nam.

He stops trying to get around me.

"Viet Nam?"

"The National Association of Mechanics. The newly formed, strictly moral governing body of your entire profession, headquartered in Lug Wrench, Ohio. Do you want to be expelled, Rayno? Never allowed to work, again? Your toolbox impounded and your name spat out with contempt by ethical grease monkeys for time eternal?"

His eyes fall into his mouth.

"Oh, mercy, no!"

I nab his shirt shoulders and yank him to me. I'm the tough cop of my daydreams.

"Then tweet, punk. Tweet like a tweety bird."

"It was Lynette!! She called, way back when, and said if the ka-jarta came in, I could fix the car, but not to tell you, but to pretend I was still ka-jarta seekin, cause you was brain-warped again and was goin off to be a porn star and I knew what a den of vipers that could be cause I had a porn semi-star cousin and she got genital herpes and now she's the Elephant Man in her groin, so when the part came in, I did what she wanted to save your crotch, and then, yesterday she called again and said I should call back and say the car was fixed, cause you ain't loonie no more, but by the glaze in your eyes, I ain't so sure about that."

I stand there, holding the trembling fool for what seems an hour.

"On the plus side, she's runnin real good."

Good and fast. Arranging her Howdee rocks, I see she sees Saaby's dust ball rolling toward her. Or maybe it's the smoke from my ears. She fast-walks for the house, as, before the car stops, I'm out of it. She throws over her shoulder, as she yanks open the door:

"Don't be hasslin me. I'm post-tobacco crazy."

I instantaneously de-materialize, then re-materialize

in the house, as she enters.

"Were you ever going to tell me the truth?"

"No harm, no foul, Quinlan."

She stomps down the hall, toward her room.

"Wrong. Harm. Foul."

She enters the room. Me too.

"This is more than a lie, Lynette. This is abduction by deception."

"Don't legalize me. I saved you from the heartbreak of herpes."

She roots in a dresser drawer.

"You promised me. You gave me your word you would not do precisely what, by my calculations...the very same day...you went and did."

"Probably genital warts, too."

She slams the drawer, opens another one.

"You're in cahoots with Lem, aren't you? Keeping me here, until I give in and become sheriff."

"Right, Quinlan. You figured us out. We got nothin better to do than co-conspire against you."

"Aha! You admit it."

"You got your car, Franco. Let it go"

"Oh, you want that. But, no, I'm not going to be

controlled by any of you, anymore. I'm taking my life back."

"You didn't have a life til this family gave you one."

She opens a nightstand drawer, pushes stuff around.

"This wasn't a family til I made it one. And this is what I get for it."

She turns on me.

"Jesus freakin christ. I was bein your friend."

"No. No. Because even after I decided against the porn business, you didn't tell me the truth, did you?"

"I…forgot."

"Forgot? Please. You kept me here because you want me. You want me so bad."

"Me? Want you?"

"But you didn't have the balls to come out and just say it."

"Listen, slim, even though you could do one hell of a lot worse than this pretty damn sweet family, I got two dildos and a Dolph Lundgren workout tape, so who needs your midget sausage?"

"Oh, that's class."

"And, Big Ears, you asked me if you could stay around, so who wants who?"

"Don't flatter yourself, Aerosol Head. I specifically said I would stay 'until I decided where to go,' but you decided to decide for me."

"In your dreams. I am off men for life plus 20 years, and even if I wasn't, you'd make me wanna be."

"Well, I am off *everybody* for life, plus…another life. You're so heinous you transcend the space-time barrier."

"Bite me, Quinlan!"

"Oh, that's a fresh epithet. Bite me, too."

"You know what? Why don't you just get in your shitty Swiss car, 'n go off to wherever you think is so much better'n here?"

"Oh, I'm going, baby. I am so going."

"Who needs your unappreciative, whiny, man ass? Go."

"First thing in the morning. Because your sleazy manipulations have invalidated everything I've felt while here. You have demolished any trust that I innocently thought existed between us. It's all been one giant, goddam lie."

We both hold our ground. She spots what she's been searching for. A pack of smokes, jammed between the headboard and the wall. She snatches them. She hesitates. She crumples the pack and flips it out the window. Despite the moment, I'm proud of her.

"Tidy your space before you go."

She walks out of the room.

I would've gotten the hell out of here, immediately, but there was the pause-buttoned, yet ongoing question of where to go. I stomped back to my stall and tried to come up with some reasonable possibilities... Tierra Del Fuego ... Kuala Lumpur ... Jersey City. But I was so agitated, so enraged, I couldn't concentrate. I needed to vent. I wanted extended seething time. I had earned it. I was entitled to it. I was going to have it. I paced. Stomped. You can't trust anyone. People are liars and connivers and will use you to get what they want, because that's how they're made. Bud used me. Lynette used me. I let them. What a sap I've been. You're alone, all alone, in this hard place and the sooner you accept it the better or you'll be nothing but a pawn in others' sick games, forever. Let me say it, again. Alone. The only real sex? Masturbation. The only real game? Solitaire. That's how it is, and I won't be forgetting it any time soon. Oh, and to my loving, absent all my life parents, should they happen to catch this from Radio Free Branson, with your "love is everything" crap: Love is a joke. Love is a lie. Love is a hook we hold onto…sentimental tripe…to delude us into believing this life has anything approximating meaning, which it doesn't. If you two had been around another five years…no, two…you'd 've been sticking forks in each other at the kitchen table and taking turns kidnapping me. No, I tried to fall for it. I tried to buy the fantasy, but the fact is, there's nothing, nothing but me, myself and I. So, that's it. I'll just go someplace and masturbate and play solitaire til I croak. Well…even in my aggrieved state that sounds pretty boring. Okay, how's this? There's nothing but mindless, pointless, sensory experience. Sex, food, parties…sex. Sure. Why not? Wallpaper that big hole with total, mind-numbing decadence. Become the white Dennis Rodman. Get a tattoo on my chest. A big zero with a question mark inside it. Yeah. That's for me. Okay, got something happening, now. But, where to go. Where to go. Oh! Oh, yeah. Oh, yeah. Lightbulb, yeah. Where else does one head to when he knows a lifelong, non-stop party is the best revenge? Where can one who has given up all hope mingle with an entire metropolis of similar-minded, damned souls? That's right, baby. You know where I mean. Vegas! Las Vegas. Las Vegas, Nevada, USA. Debauchery City. Desperation Row. My next and final destination. Oh, man. This is so hot. What an idea. Ooh, ooh, I'll become a player. A high roller. Cold hearted. Soulless. Empty eyes. Figuring the odds and making sure they're on my side, always. Shiny suits. Hermes ties. Showgirls on arms. Big BMW. Sorry, Saaby, you don't fit the new me. Oh, baby! When I stride into a casino, people will see me and nudge each other. Penn and Teller shake my hand. Jimmy the bartender's got my "usual" waiting. Groupies gather round me at the high stakes baccarat table, as my icily cool demeanor and logarithmic mind shatter the other gamers and carry me to another six-figure night of winnings. And, after building up a bankroll of several mil...figure a month...I'll go to phase two. Build my own casino. Yeah, yeah, yeah. Call it...Hades. Big neon flames, everywhere. Waitresses with tails and horns. Fleece the unwashed masses out of their tank tops and shower clogs. Take their fuckin rent money, heeheehee. And another thing. Going back to tell off Bud? Not. I'm going to *be* Bud. Vegas

Bud. Bud Plus. I'll take every corrupt, rapacious lesson he ever taught me and apply it to becoming the biggest bigshot The Strip has ever seen. More casinos. More. I'll turn Steve Wynn into Steve Lose. It'll be my own personal Monument to Nothing. Because that's what life is. You walk around for a while, you drop. I've always known it, but now I'm embracing it. Relishing it. Reveling in it. Yes, yes, yes. The real me is finally showing up. I'm going down into the hellfire. Below the bowels, where I belong. I can take it. I can take anything, because I expect nothing. That's the key. Nothing. Not the zen nothing, but the nothing nothing. The nothing ventured, nothing gained, nothing lost, nothing to lose, nothing. Zero. Zip. Snake eyes. Nothing, nothing, nothing, nothing, nothing. And I'll have more than anyone!

I sleep without dreaming, then wake rested and exhilarated by the new and worse me. I clean my area, while considering just what kind of oversized, shiny, Vegas Guy medallion I'll choose to have dangling from my open-shirted chest. I also wonder if you can have more chest hair implanted, and does it have that picket fence look? I grab all my belongings, which consist of:

My laptop. I smirk. Cruelly, I hope. Moose is a bit crooked on the wall. I straighten him, so he won't feel the world is sideways, even though it is. I walk away.

Determined to do things right, I gather the troops in the living room, for farewells. Not everyone. Henrik demonstrates his abiding affection for me, by not being here. He, apparently, rose early to go gather klonchkrock, some desert root that, in addition to being the only two-syllable word I know that has three "k's," he grinds up and peppers into all his preparations. It's only fitting that a man who never really knew I was here, would now be unaware I'd left. But the nuclear trio is at hand, and I'm feeling so personally strong and clear of cynical purpose, at the moment, that I have no hesitance in pretending to express the affection I don't have for them. I tell Eddie how much I respect his fighting his way back from the depths. I muss his hair and give him a quick hug, then hang onto him tightly, just so, you know, he won't think I don't care about him, even though I don't. I jokingly say to Diana that perhaps I'll call her for radio therapy someday. She takes my hands and says:

"Follow the iambic pentameter of your soul."

Then informs me that she now wants a TV show. Syndicated.

Lynette's off to the side, arms crossed, her face pulled in like an under-inflated football. I step to her.

"Lynette, despite things said and done, I choose to part on amicable terms."

I offer my hand. She stares a bullet into the space between my eyes, swallows hard and says:

"You are such an asshole."

"Okay, that's friendly enough."

I pick up my laptop. I give a mini wave.

"Goomba."

I clear my throat. Despite her villainy, I admit, it's a bit hard to see Lynette hurting.

"I mean…good-bye."

"Who's that?"

Asks Eddie, looking out the window. I turn. A face, peering in. I utter, calmly:

"That would be Bud."

I say nothing else. What is there to say? Surprisingly, I'm not even surprised. My erstwhile mentor spots me. He pounds the windowpane a la Dustin Hoffman in *The Graduate*.

"Who's that yahoo?"

Lynette steps to the window.

"Hey! You break it you bought it, podner."

Bud disappears.

BAM!

He shoulders the door down. Ridiculous. It's never locked. Letting me know he's a trifle peeved, I suppose. But I'm not there. Or here. I'm…somewhere else.

"I'm gonna rip you apart with my own hands!"

I'm guessing he means me.

"Code blue, kids! Code blue. Madman in the house!"

He charges me. I'm a statue, but Lynette's on him, throwing a headlock on the enraged mogul.

"This must be Quinlan's arch-enemy, who poisoned his soul and sent him crazy into the night."

"Bastard!"

Exclaims Diana, as she and Eddie grab onto the flailing CEO.

"Work him over, children, the same as Turpin."

They commence pounding Bud. But I'm…outdoors, I think. Go on, Bud. Punch me. Nothin there. Paul has left the building. But Bud doesn't realize this. He's dragging the three of them toward me.

"What about my girl, you pansy pussy? Nobody jilts Bud's girl."

"Hang on, kids. He wants Quinlan's blood!"

"Nobody hurts Quinlan!"

That was Diana, as she kicked Bud in the ribs.

"Ufff."

"That's my girl."

But Bud keeps coming, inexorably, forward.

"He's getting loose. Should I bite him, mom?"

"Permission granted, Eddie."

"Awwwww!"

The country? Am I in the country? I smell trees. I hear water. Hmm. It's nice. Bucolic.

"Nobody messes with Quinlan!"

And Diana punts Bud, again.

"Ammm! Ammm!

He falls to a knee. The Three Musketeers are jackals. Punching him, gouging, ripping, tearing. Amazingly, Bud laughs.

"Haaaaa!"

And then, with three humans hanging on him, that Fortune 500 manimal begins to, remarkably, rise. He froths out:

"I get up. I always get up!"

He loves this. He thrives, at last in his true Darwinian element.

"Graaawww!"

He roars and takes a step. It's beautiful, somehow. He's lice, toe jam, but you gotta grudgingly respect the perfection of his evilness.

"He's crazy. Mom. Get your gun."

"Can't let go, son. Grab his legs, Diana."

Diana tries to. Bud kicks her. In the head. And, I'm…where is this? Oh. The cemetery. And everybody's comforting me and there's flowers and a minister and two coffins and I'm holding my nose, because Aunt Ina just cut one and then I can't see so well because something seems to be clouding my eyes. And then I jolt with a spasm like I'm giving birth and I buckle with something close to pain but different because pain is a presence. This is an absence. This is empty. A nameless never again and I can't do anything but endure it. Endure it and go on, anyway. Hope for another chance. And then I see Diana, half-out on the floor, moaning, and the others fighting for me. Not with my voice, but from some other place deep inside me and long ago, I scream:

"You can't have them, too!"

And Bud freezes. Eddie and Lynette, Christmas icicles, hang from him. He turns on me. The temperature drops 50 degrees, but I don't feel it. He's lost it. Whatever he had over me once, it's gone. Long gone. As gone as disco. As gone as hair on Rayno's head.

"Try kicking a man, you pussy prick!"

He flings Eddie and Lynette like they're dandruff.

"When I see one, I will."

He takes a step. I swing. He ducks. I swing, again. I graze his greasy head. I grab his skull. I head butt it. Not a great idea. I see stars, he just grins. He smashes me in the chest, as hard as he can.

"Gnuk!"

Does his fist come out the other side? I can't breathe. It doesn't hurt, though. No. Wait a second. It does. Yeah. Here comes the pain. A flaming spear in my chest. I'm dizzy. I'm going to fall. No. Luckily, Bud grabs my hair. Thanks, Bud. As if to show me how to do it right, he knees me in the face.

"Merp."

I see orange birds. I can't move. No, I can. I can fall

down. I do. Lynette gymnastically flips off the floor, hoists a ceramic bust of Richard Petty and crowns King B with it. No effect. He lifts her up and body slams her to the floor. She bounces, once, then doesn't do anything. Here comes Eddie! Head butt. It's a head butt extravaganza! No. Bud catches that spunky, recovering alcoholic kid's noggin with a perfectly timed elbow. Eddie stops. Cold. He shivers to his knees, cradling his poor skull to keep it from falling apart. Now, only Bud is upright. His hair is standing on end. His shirt is out, ripped. One shoe off. Blood spurts out an eye. He's in heaven. Orgasmic. He makes guttural sounds, as he eyes his true prey. Unable to raise a hand, I whimper. Bud froths at the mouth and gets me just so, in his sights.

"Now. I'm gonna kill you with my own hands!"

He was always a micro-manager. This might be a good time to leave. Why can't I walk? I try. I take a step. My foot stays where it was. Hey, foot. Come on. Bud slides toward me, in slow motion. Foot! Please! Nope. I'm epoxied. This is it. The moment of no more me. I want to see them one more time. The three. Where are they?

He sinks his meaty paws in my neck. Deep. Deeper. I can't even offer token resistance. Deeper. Deeper. Bud always gets what he wants. My lungs become a vacuum cleaner's bag when you turn it off, but I keep my eyes open. I visually pull back. A camera lens. Give myself a broader view. Paul-a-Vision. A wide shot. There they are. All of them. Scattered. Playing cards in the wind. So hurt. Paul, Paul. See what they did for you? Aw geez, Paulie, couldn't you have figured out one thing, just one, in time?

Deeper. Deeper. Salsa on his breath. Lynette comes around. She tries to stand. She can't. She reaches out an arm to me. I try to tell her with my eyes, but they're closing. Closing. Bud's grunting, leaning on me. Pushing me down. Personally escorting me to hell…gloating that, Hades being his eventual destination too, we'll surely meet again and he can then re-murder me, every day, non-stop, for all eternity. More pressure on my neck. Will it snap? More. Down. Down. Who played third base? Down. I'm a handyman. Underwater, with mom and dad. Handy-dandy-andy man. See ya, world. I'll be leaving now. Thanks for parks. And the Alps. Harvey Keitel.

Chocolate. I'll even forgive you for prevent defenses. It was mostly a mess but, god how I loved it.

"Grnga."

My last word. Appropriate. Except, I didn't say it. So, who did?

"Grnga."

Oh, Bud. He's…elevating. Then he scoots away from me, as if he's on the moving sidewalk at the airport, going the other way. Wow. Something painful slices my throat. What is that? Air? Hey, Henrik's got him. Oh, hi, Henrik. Get some good Klonchkrock? He's dangling Bud in the air, in a cool, one-hand thing. Bud hovers. Hunh. He's got eeny-teeny feet. They flail about and it looks funny and I try to laugh but only snot comes out. Oh, oh. If ever there were a match for Super Kraut, it's Bad B. He thumbs Henrik's eye. Takes more than that for Henrik to let go. So, Bud, master of improvisation that he is, even while levitated, rips Henrik's chest hair. Henrik yowls. Bud keeps yanking. What a match. Better than Flair and Hogan. Whoo! Henrik dinosaur wails. Bud yanks some more. Henrik turns, slowly, a revolving statue, bleating as he does. He faces the wall, ten or twelve feet from it. Bud wrings another thatch of silver fuzz out, victoriously.

"Klm! Klrnnmoe!"

He crows and goes for more. Henrik's false teeth fly out. He starts slowly. Slowly, moving forward. Did you ever see a high jumper when they begin their move to the bar? Steadily, evenly, in control, but building tremendous momentum. Go, Henrik, go! The last two steps, Henrik the Great is a blur as he inserts Bud into the wall. I do mean *into*. Four inches. This is too much for even The Great Asshole. Kayo City. Eight, nine, ten. Get the smelling salts.

My foot moves. It moves, again. One step too many. I fall down. In a mere three minutes, I'm back up. Shit. Ankle's twisted. Lynette's rising. Showing some nipple again, through her torn t-shirt. The kids are dazed, but grinning.

"Hell, children, was that fun, or what?"

They all cheer. I do, too, spitting up a tooth. Henrik, wanting to share in the merriment, goes all out and puts his hands on his hips.

"You alive, Quinlan?"

I rasp.

"No, but I'm kicking."

Sccllcchh.

"Kids, what's the injury report?"

"Busted nose, ma."

"It'll give you character, Diana. Eddie?"

Sccllcchh.

"Separated shoulder, I think."

"No prob. We'll pop it back."

"What's that?"

"What's what, Quinlan?"

Sccclllccchhh!

"That."

"That would be the sound I told you we didn't have to worry about, 'less we heard, and we're hearin it. Guess our hasslin upset Mr. Rock."

Sccllcchh.

The rock?!

And it jerks. An earthquake's worth. Everything's sideways.

"Let's go, children. Hurry, but don't rush. Plenty a time."

But, there isn't. Lynette and the kids have barely gotten to their feet, when...

Sccclllchchchchhh.

The ceiling drops. Thud. Eight inches. Stop. Eddie dives out a long window that's now short. Diana and Lynette are…hunh, they're gone, too. I see Bud, a crumpled wad of paper on what used to be the floor. I take a step toward him. Okay. That hurts.

"Henrik. Give me a hand with him."

But Henrik's pre-occupied, staring upward.

"Henrik?"

Sccllcchh.

Henrik's daring the rock, with a sneer.

"Gehen sie aus. Mach schnell!"

Sccllcchh.

Wham! Another ten inches. A big section of ceiling comes down. No, it's not ceiling, it's roof. See the weathervane? Ho. Where's Bud? Oops. Under it. Mini-Gucci's sticking out. Can I dig him out in time?

Sccllcchhcchh!

Now the rock pokes its nose into view. Well, boss, I'm sorry. Time seems to be of the essence here, and surely you, of all people, understand about looking out for number one, and all that, so, best of luck, which you'll need because you're on your own, here. I hop. Pain. I hop, again. I'm making for what's left of the doorway.

"Henrik. Come on."

Scccclllllcccchhhhhh!

And the house is tossed for loose change. I'm down, back up. The doorway's not there anymore. It's on the ceiling. I spot a crack in the wall. An oval hole. A wooden vagina. I hobble for it. Somehow, defying every law of physics, Henrik hasn't been budged. He's not moving. He's right where he was, staring the rock down, while looking up.

"Henrik!"

I bunny hop across the tiny space. Hop. Anh! Hop. The rock releases. Hophophop. It just lets go. All the way. Hop. Shit. Too far. Curtain City. At least it'll be quick. Light. Dark. See ya. Here she comes...she's coming...au revoir...ces't la vie...except, Henrik, lifting his arms like a reborn sinner at a Billy Graham Revival...catches the rock. He catches it! With his hands. His knees buckle, but...he holds it above him, as if it's a record setting weight he's lifted and is holding aloft for all the world to see. Despite the situation, I stop, flat-footed. Amazed. In awe. I want to...I don't know...applaud.

"Go! Take care a dem!"

I get scared, again. I somehow take two big steps, hurl myself into the wall-hole. A force grabs me. Suctions. I'm food scraps, wiggling down the drain. Down. Sinking. Swirling. Wait. I'm not. No sinking. Dragging. It's Lynette. And Diana. And Eddie, with his good arm. They're hauling me away, away. I'm on my back, and outside and I see the pretty sky that's always bluer here than anywhere else, and I'm bouncing along quite nicely and I don't even mind the burrs that are ripping my ass. And…hey, I see the house. There, it is. No. No, it isn't. Where's it going? Geez, the walls are crumbling, one side at a time. Almost in rhythm. Plunk. Plunk. Plunk. Plunk. All down. No more house. Just Henrik, in the middle of what used to be it. Atlas, he is. Still hoisting the sad, lost world on his hard-working, inarticulate shoulders. He doesn't see me. His face is contorted, eyes closed. He might be grunting. I don't know, I can't hear. Does he know I got out? He should know. Ooh. He starts to get shorter. My god, he's being driven into the ground. The rock lowers. One notch. Then, another. Short, Henrik. Shorter. He's buried to his waist. I shout:

"Henrik! Henrik!"

My family stops dragging me. We're next to the Howdee rocks, which don't look as kitschy as I'd imagined. They're sweet. Welcoming. The others turn to see what I'm yelling at. Now, Henrik's in up to his chest. I rasp, again:

"Henrik! Henrik!"

He sees me! His head is nodding. It, and two forearms, are the only parts of him above ground, but his noggin's bobbing. It's bobbing, like Rayno's Garth Brooks doll. He's...oh, dear. He's grinning, showing the teeth he doesn't have. Yeah. Big grin. He's always happy when he's working...when he's "helfen." Notch. His head's starting to go. I know about six words of German. I quickly call one out:

"Ausgezeichnet!"

*

You know the rest. Almost. I did go back to L.A., to clean up unfinished business. But now, the business was Lindsay. If I'd done anything unconscionable in taking off, it was in not having the decency to consider her feelings. I owed her, at the least, the four-lettered opportunity to righteously tell me off. But she wasn't angry. Freed from the Bud yoke, she had changed, dramatically. She wasn't done up in the showy designer outfits her father always insisted she wear so people would know he was rich. She was wearing jeans. A top. Tennies. She was smiling. Happy. As we munched burgers, she talked about things. Real things. Art. Politics. Stem cells. She was smart. Lindsay had a brain. She was curious, interested, interesting. We talked and talked. About our future. Our past. Parents. No parents. Then, we stopped talking. We sat, quietly and considered. And Lindsay said:

"I'm glad he's dead."

"You should know, right before he tried to choke me to death, he mentioned your name."

"I'm really glad he's dead."

"In his own, twisted, fatherly way, he was trying to avenge your honor."

"I am...oh, so very glad he's dead."

I sigh.

"Yeah. I'm glad, too."

✳

My head's almost as big as Lem's and with some toilet paper lining, that crisp man's man's...even if the man's a woman...Stetson fits just fine. I shine the star every night and try to live up to the code our sheriff emeritus left me with: To be fair, to not shoot unless shot at and to never, ever order the frijoles negros at Panchito's Taqueria.

I bought her house. We'd already been living there, as she took us in the night the rock fell and wouldn't accept a penny. It was the end of an era on the rainy day that great bear-woman took leave of us, with Kitty, in her trusty Nissan. I'm not ashamed to say I shed a tear, even though Lem swore she'd come visit, but hasn't and probably won't because that's how those things go.

Luther offered to imbue our new home with a helpful animal spirit. Alas, most of his favorite creatures had already been used and he was reluctant to double-imbue, as the gods might get confused. Then, he noticed Moose hanging on the wall above the sofa. I had managed to salvage the big stuffed fellow from the rubble, minus one antler and his nose. Luther decided Moose were good for domestic tranquility, as he had never seen, in all his years, two Moose arguing, so he Moose'd us and I suppose it's worked because, while Lynette and I do, sometimes, lock horns, it's always short-lived and we invariably make up by nuzzling each other's snouts.

Diana's at USC. She's had a fine college career. Her student radio call-in show, "Mind Your Mind," was so popular it was picked up by MTV, so we get to see her dispense wise beyond her years advice every Saturday afternoon and then jump up and down a lot, in a thong bikini, when she emcees "Gangsta Volleyball" on Sundays.

Eddie's in the tenth grade. On the varsity basketball team. A not bad point guard, who's at his best in crunch time. He still asks me to help with his homework once in a while and I'm happy to do so.

We, the folks, spend our time quietly, or as quietly as possible, when one of us is Lynette. Occasionally, on summer evenings when it cools down a bit, we'll take a ride in Saaby. We often find our way over to the rock, which is still in one piece where it fell. We may climb it and watch the sunset. Or make love up there, to let Henrik know everything's still fine between us and he wasn't croquet staked in vain. Not too long ago a cat showed up on the rock while we were having a beer. I counted its toes. One, two, three, four five, six, seven.

Is there a plan, after all? Was everything that happened to me pre-ordained or just circumstance? What I've learned is…I don't know. I can't know. These things are beyond our mind's capacity of comprehension. Sure, lots of people think they know, but trust me, they're just guessing. What is true and can be verified, is that this consciousness is short and fraught with peril, and the good in it is merely on loan. We're all on TST, Temporary Standard Time. How to spend our precious, parenthetical moments between nothingnesses is the relevant question.

Dad was right. Lately, I've been singing *The Paulie Song* a lot. Remember? Dad said I'd recall it when I needed it.

Paul sings, softly…

"I love you like a little, I love you like a lot.

You're the fish upon my griddle, you're my baby tater tot.

It's a pitch right down the middle, it's a little that's a lot.

It is peace and joy my little boy. In the end it's all we got."

Is that simplistic? Maybe. But you have to let go and just make a stand sometime, right? You have to say, this is who I am. This is what is important because something inside me says it is. You have to believe in the possibility, at least, of your heart knowing things you don't. With some trust and nurturing, it might even speak to you, after a while. It might say things, low and soft, such as: We must let ourselves be held, good and tight, despite how undeserving we know we are. Laugh as hard and as long as we can at the holes inside us. Forgive. Climb into that chasm, which is bathed in glorious, tear-stained light and the smell of the desert morning for as long as something pre-ordained wants it to be, and then…dance. For the hell of it. For spite. With elegance and panache and personal aplomb. With Argentine style. We must all dance under the rock until the music stops.

ABOUT THE AUTHOR

Dennis Koenig is an Emmy and Writers Guild of America nominated writer/producer. His many credits include the award-winning series *M*A*S*H* and *Anything But Love*. Dennis lives in Santa Barbara with his wife, writer/producer Wendy Kout, who is almost as chatty as their cat, Gracie Allen.

Made in the USA
Las Vegas, NV
20 November 2020